RETURN OF BLUE WOLF

Sequel to - "SEARCH FOR BLUE WOLF"

by Tarrie A. McBride

Inquiries and Book Orders should be addressed to:

Great Writers Media
Email: info@greatwritersmedia.com
Phone: 877-600-5469

ISBN: 979-8-89175-098-2 (sc)
ISBN: 979-8-89175-097-5 (ebk)

EXTERIOR J&T RANCH OUTSIDE OF WHISKEY
CREEK, SOUTH DAKOTA- 1891 -DAY

Kan Wu, The Chinese cook (Cookie) rides up to the ranch in a
buckboard bringing supplies. He heads toward the rifle and pistol
fire out back. BAM! BAM! BAM! POP! POP! BAM! BAM!

COOKIE

Mista' MacRoy! Mista' MacRoy!

John MacRoy, his son Tim MacRoy and Big Ben are there
with four new cowpokes: PONCHO GARCIA, a Mexican
quick shot artist, Rod MCCULLA, an Australian Cowboy and
sharpshooter, HANS BECKER a German gunsmith and MAJOR
WILLS, a retired US Army officer. They're firing at targets in
the shape of dinosaurs. BAM! BAM! POP! POP! BAM!

JOHN MACROY

Hold your fire! Hold your fire!

Cookie pulls up to John.

COOKIE

I got all the supplies we need for three to four weeks.

JOHN MACROY

That's a beautiful thing Cookie. Welcome back.

The firing range consists of an open plain with posts and pulleys.
The target operator makes metal cutouts of dinosaurs that
travel or pop up across the field. This bunker worker controls
the targets. Poncho Garcia and Rod McCulla are now up.

JOHN MACROY

All ready on the firing line?!

PONCHO GARCIA

Ready!

ROD MCCULLA

Ready mate!

JOHN MACROY

Are you ready Tim?

TIM MACROY

(from distance)

Ready!

JOHN MACROY

Okay. Tim let them go.

Poncho has two colt 45 revolvers and McCulla has a Winchester rifle. A six-foot metal dinosaur rises up about thirty feet out. POP! POP! BAM! BAM! POP! POP! BAM! They fill the target with lead. Another target pops up about fifty feet out. BAM! BAM! POW! POW! POP! BLAM! They in turn fill that dino' with holes.

JOHN MACROY

Hold your fire! Pretty good gents! Remember these beasts will be eight to ten times larger than these targets. They›ll eat you like a chicken drumstick given the chance. Who›s got the big guns?

BIG BEN

Mister Mac', they be right here!

Ben has one of the factory-made dinosaur guns designed by Johns' friend, Dr. Gatling, who invented the Gatling gun. These are sleeker, but are still heavy for an average shooter.

JOHN MACROY

Ben, give it a go. You know how to use it.

BIG BEN

Yes Sah! I do!

JOHN MACROY

Tim! Are you ready with these pop-up targets?

Tim shouts from a distance of about sixty
feet from the cement blind.

TIM MACROY

All set! Ready when you are!

JOHN MACROY

Alright son, let 'em go!

A dino' target pops up on the far left. Ben fires BAM! BAM!
BAM! BAM! BAM! BAM! Only pieces remain on the string.

JOHN MACROY

Bloody good! Nice shooting Ben!

The others cheer.

EVERYONE

YAHOO! YIPEE! WAHOO!

JOHN MACROY

Ben... You're the best when it comes to these Gatling
rifles. Lord knows we wouldn't have made it back home
without your talent behind that pea-shooter.

ROD MCCULLA

Aye Mista Mac, would ya' give this Ausey a try at
shootin' the lizads with that Gatlin' repeata'?

JOHN MACROY

That's why you're here. I've heard you're good.

ROD MCCULLA

Just need a try or two to get used to this Dingo shoota'.

Rod inspects the slide, safety, trigger and clip.

JOHN MACROY

(shouting)

OK son, are you ready?!

TIM MACROY

I'm ready!

JOHN MACROY

McCulla are you ready?!

ROD MCCULLA

Ready!

JOHN MACROY

OK! Son let 'em go!

A five-foot Triceratops dinosaur is pulled by a rope traversing the ground toward a pole at the opposite end of the field. McCulla commences firing in a strafing pattern that cuts the beast in half. BAM! BAM! BAM! BAM! BAM! BAM! He then shoots back the other direction. The target is totally demolished.

EVERYONE

Wahoo! Yipee!

ROD MCCULLA

That's some weapon, Mr. MacRoy!

JOHN MACROY

Oh, you'll find a use for it. I guarantee it. OK! let's get two shooters
up on the firing line...How about Major Wills and Hans Becker.
Take these Winchester rifles and give it a go at some pop-up targets.

They move up to their positions with rifles.

JOHN MACROY

All ready on the firing line?!

MAJOR WILLS

Ready!

HANS BECKER

Ready!

JOHN MACROY

(shouting)

OK! Tim let "em go!

A target pops up twenty-five feet out to the right. BANG!
BANG! POP! POP! BANG! BANG! PLINK! POP! BANG!
BANG! Another target pops up fifty feet out on the right.
BANG! POP! POP! BANG! PLINK! BLAM! POW! POW!

JOHN MACROY

OK! OK! Gents that's great shooting. There's nary a
one of ya' that isn't qualified to be on board.

A voice comes from behind the cement blind on the firing range.

TIM MACROY

Hey Pop! Don't forget about your favorite son! I deserve a turn!

JOHN MACROY

Aye, that you do Laddie. You're next.

BIG BEN

I'll take over for him out there Mr. Mac.

JOHN MACROY

OK Ben...Come on down here son!

As Tim approaches, they see riders in the distance. As they get closer, they see Sioux braves on horseback. It's Blue Wolf, Painted Horse and four other braves. They all arrive at the firing line, as does Tim.

JOHN MACROY

Greetings Blue Wolf and Sioux braves!

Raven Feathers interprets for his Sioux brothers.

RAVEN FEATHERS

Blue Wolf thanks you for your offer for the rifles. It will help us to provide minetonka...how you say...buffalo.

MAJOR WILLS

Indians? Rifles?

BIG BEN

Major Wills, these Injuns saved our lives when we were surrounded by 'dem giant lizards. They's friends.

MAJOR WILLS

Did you remember what happened just four years ago at Little Big Horn? We should be rounding up these "Red" bastards and putting them on reservations.

JOHN MACROY

Major Wills you didn't even get a chance to meet our
good friends Blue Wolf, Painted Horse, and braves.

MAJOR WILLS

I don›t care to. I can't be a part of a rag-tag Indian loving
crew that›s contributing to the demise of the white man.

TIM MACROY

Major Wills, they saved my dad, Ben, Cookie
and me. If they hadn't showed up…

The Major walks over to his horse and mounts as he interrupts Tim.

MAJOR WILLS

Son, you're too green to know which end is up.
They'll lie, cheat, steal and eventually kill you.

JOHN MACROY (upset)

Major, you've been too busy warring to see their merits! If not for
Indians the Pilgrims would have starved some 140 years ago.

MAJOR WILLS

Don't be deceived. They're snakes waiting to bite you!

JOHN MACROY

GET OFF MY LAND! PREACH YOUR
HATRED ELSEWHERE!!

MAJOR WILLS

This is not the end MacRoy! You'll see!

JOHN MACROY

You're not in the US Army any more, Citizen
Wills. Be careful with your threats!

He rides away shouting back.

MAJOR WILLS

I see bad things for you MacRoy! REAL BAD!

BIG BEN

Should I shoot his ass Mr. MacRoy?

JOHN MACROY

I wouldn't waste the bullet. He'll get what's
coming to him in due time.

PONCHO GARCIA

And maybe sooner.

TWO DAYS LATER

EXITING J&T RANCH TO THE BLACK
HILLS -CONTINUOUS DAY

Two large covered wagons loaded with supplies head out the ranch
entrance. The J&T Ranch sign sways and creeks in the wind.

JOHN MACROY

Come on gents. Get a move on. Follow our
Indian guides. They've been there before.

TUFFY (small family dog) barking wildly out of a partially
closed window. Tuffy doesn't want to be left behind.

Arf! Arf! Bark! Bark! Bark! Bark!

TIM MACROY

Dad, we forgot Tuffy! We gotta' stop! I"ll get him. While
we're stopped, did you remember the spare wagon parts
and the backup guns and ammo? And food?

JOHN MACROY

That I did Laddie. We've got all the tools and parts to
maintain our wagons, we've got food- beef jerky, slab bacon,
potatoes, eggs coffee and fruit to boot! Right Cookie?!
Cookie pops his head out of the wagon.

COOKIE

You did Mr. Mac. I told you what I bring.
Food for 3 weeks is good, yes?

JOHN MACROY

Real good Cookie. I'm sure glad you're with us, my Chinese friend.

COOKIE

Me too. I get food ready for first stop. How long before we stop?

JOHN MACROY

It may take six hours to get there. We'll stop at noon for chow and
feed the animals. We 'll inspect all our weapons at that time too.

HANS BECKER

Good. I can clean some of the weapons. Take
them apart and fine tune them.

JOHN MACROY

We might even camp there overnight. That's about four
hours away. I want to sleep our first night on this side
of time. OK you all. Let's head out! Gitty-up!

BIG BEN

I hear ya' boss. Let's get to our spot on this side of the world.
I don't want to wake up to 'dem giant lizards on their side.

Rod McCulla rides his horse closer.

ROD MCCULLA

I heard ya' talkin 'bout the giant lizads (lizards) that have a taste
for humans. I've eaten giant lizads before. Salties taste good!

TIM MACROY

What's a Salty?

ROD MCCULLA

A salt water crocodile. I've killed 'em four meters long.

COOKIE

I help you cook. Chinese are the best cooks.

The caravan of cowboys and Indians moves toward the
portal. Armed to the hilt they're ready for adventure.

HANS BECKER

Do you think we have enough fire power against these huge beasts?

JOHN MACROY

I believe so. We just have to watch out for Dinosaur ambushes.

Rod pulls something peculiar out of his saddle pack.

ROD MCCULLA

I'm hopin' to use this on a smalla' one.

He holds up a boomerang.

JOHN MACROY

What have you got there?

ROD MCCULLA

It's a boomerang. Aboriginals use it to hunt
'roos. Kangaroos. Watch this.

He stands up in the saddle and hurls it. It starts end over end
and turns laterally and comes back full circle to the thrower.

EVERYONE

Yahoo! Woopie!

BIG BEN

'Dat be some flyin' piece of weapon you gots there Mista McCulla.

PONCHO GARCIA

Aye carumba! I have to see this again.

JOHN MACROY

Look out! (he points to the ground 12 feet away) Rattlesnake!

ROD MCCULLA

I got it. Hold still.

Rod stands up in his saddle. Looks for an angle and
throws in a weird direction, away from the snake. It
turns around low and clips the snakes head off.

EVERYONE

You betcha! great job! Holy Smoke!

JOHN MACROY

I'm sure glad you're on our team. Ok, everyone let's keep a
move on. We want to get to the passage way before dark.

FOUR HOURS LATER

The Indians slow the wagons to view something in the distance. It's a small herd of buffalo! Blue Wolf and Raven Feathers approach John.

Blue Wolf

(Dakota Tongue)

My people hunger for meat. The iron horse hunters have killed many buffalo. Look! These will give food and clothing. Let us stop here, for a short while. Raven Feathers interprets.

RAVEN FEATHERS

Blue Wolf will go with several braves and myself. We will leave Painted Horse with you to guide you. We will catch up after we take the meat to our village.

JOHN MACROY

Listen up laddies! The Indians are asking we camp here for the night. They want to hunt those buffalo to feed their village. We'll get meat too. Everyone OK with that?

BIG BEN

Dat's OK by me.

ROD MCCULLA

Sure... the aboriginals need some meat too.

HANS BECKER

Fine.

PANCHO GARCIA

Esta Bueno. It's good.

TIM MACROY

Can we hunt with them?

JOHN MACROY

I can't see why a couple of ya' couldn't go. Mr. McCulla
and Poncho, would you join in the hunt?

TIM MACROY

Me too Dad?

JOHN MACROY

Son I would rather you...

ROD MCCULLA

Mr. Mac I'll go with the boy and watch over him.

JOHN MACROY

Alright, take your rifles and son take your six shooters.

TIM MACROY

Thanks Dad.

Cookie comes out of the wagon.

COOKIE

Here is a bag of beef jerky and some fruit.
You take and eat for energy.

RAVEN FEATHERS

We will watch over them Great one.

JOHN MACROY

We'll set up camp and wait for your return.
Make sure you're strong and fast!

COOKIE

Food and coffee will be here for your return.

They all leave. Tim waves as they ride out.

EXTERIOR MOUNTAINS AND PLAINS -DAY

About three hundred yards from the herd, Blue Wolf
points to half of the men to circle above the buffalo and
the other half to close in from below the herd.

ROD MCCULLA

Kid, stay with us riders. Don't get caught
in the middle of those buffalo.

The buffalo stampede. Four bulls charge toward the riders.

ROD MCCULLA

Look out son! Move over behind me. I'm shootin'.

Bam! Bam! Bam! One bull slides on his side, kicks up dust and
dies. Tim sees the second bull charging on their blind side.

TIM MACROY

Look Out!

BAM! BAM! BAM! BAM! This beast rears back and falls
spread eagle with his tongue hanging out for a death pose.

ROD MCCULLA

Good shootin' mate.

Two Sioux braves come alongside a prize bull. Arrows
pierce its neck and side. Blue Wolf downs the beast with
one shot to the heart from his Winchester rifle.

Blue Wolf calls a stop. The harvest is full.

BLUE WOLF

(Lakota tongue)

Four bulls of Tetonka (buffalo) are good. Take meat
and hides for the village. We take some for camp.

BIG BEN
We betta' get these buffaloes to those trees
so's we can hang and butcher 'dem.

The Braves make sleds from tree branches to drag the
meat and hides after butchering them. Two Sioux braves
launch out to bring buffalo to their village.

TWO HOURS LATER

The other hunting party of cowboys and Indians
arrives at camp dragging their surprise.

JOHN MACROY

Well, give a look here. We already had lunch two hours
ago but a buffalo steak looks mighty fine laddies.

COOKIE

I prepare chop, chop. You have steak, potatoes and
onions with biscuits and gravy. Give me one hour.

BIG BEN

I'm ready to eat some cooked or not!

JOHN MACROY

We›re not like the bloody «T› Rex we hunt. Remember, we›re
looking for a lady that brought civilization to this old «Scottsman".

TIM MACROY

Dad, I qualified as a man.... I brought down a buffalo!

JOHN MACROY

That you did Lad, and a real man you are for sure, for sure!

ONE HOUR LATER

EXT AROUND CAMPFIRE MEAL IN
"BLACK HILLS" -NIGHT
Everyone's enjoying the buffalo meat barbeque.

HANS BECKER

That was such a fine meal. Danka Schoen (thank you)

Tuffy starts barking, Arf! Arf! Arf!

TIM MACROY

Did we forget you Tuffy? Here some buffalo scraps. Love you boy.

Tim pats his head as he scarfs down the meat.

PONCHO GARCIA

Cookie the carne was good. Muchas Gracias. (Thank you)

COOKIE
Sorry, no fortune cookies.

ROD MCCULLA

That tastes almost as good as 'roo.

They all look puzzled.

ROD MCCULLA

(cont.)

Oh sorry, kangaroo meat, mates.

BIG BEN

It tastes better than those giant lizards, but they ain't bad.
I think Cookie could make anything taste good.

JOHN MACROY

Let's get a bit of shut eye. We have a big day ahead of us.
Remember it's Five hundred dollars for each man to come back
alive. Our ultimate goal ... find Virginia. Good night to ya'.
John walks over to his bed. Everyone lingers near the
campfire. They talk about the adventures that lie ahead

HANS BECKER

It is true that Mr. MacRoy pays each of us five
hundred dollars to find his fiancee and return!

BIG BEN

He paid me $250 dollars when we found the
entrance to this land of dinosaurs and two hundred
fifty when we made it out alive, last time.

PONCHO GARCIA

Aye Chihuahua! That money sure sounds good. I
could buy a nice rancho in my town in Mexico and
live like a king with mucho senioritas everywhere.

ROD MCCULLA

Oh, come on Poncho., get out

PONCHO GARCIA

Es cierta! It is the truth senior McCulla.

HANS BECKER

Are the dinosaurs very dangerous?

BIG BEN

Well, they could eat you fasta' than you could say, Black Eyed Peas. Them "T" Rex is da' meanest. Their head is bigger than two bath tubs and teeth as long as my fingers.

PONCHO GARCIA

Sancti Maria! (Holy Mary) ...and they run fast?

BIG BEN
They run as fast as a race horse!

PONCHO GARCIA

Aye carone! I hope they shoot dead mas facile, how you say ...easier.

Rod McCulla walks to the fire.

ROD MCCULLA

Hi mates! Can I join ya'?

HANS BECKER

Sure, sit down.

PONCHO GARCIA

Si, si, senor. (yes, yes Mister)

BIG BEN

Sit...Tell us about that funny stick you throw.

ROD MCCULLA

Oh, you mean me boomerang! It was invented by the aboriginal people. They hunted 'roo with it.

BIG BEN

A- bor' what did you call 'dem?

ROD MCCULLA

Aboriginals. Ben they're black people like yourself. Live
in Australia before white man ever stepped foot.

BIG BEN

And dey still got these people?

ROD MCCULLA

Still do.

BIG BEN

Dey weren't sold like Mammy and pappy
as slaves to work da cotton?

ROD MCCULLA

No sir, they're protected by the government.

PONCHO GARCIA

That boomer... why did they make that?

ROD MCCULLA

Invented the boomerang? They did to hunt 'roos...kangaroos...
creatures as big as a man and look like a jack rabbit.

PONCHO GARCIA

Aye, carumba, that must be some ugly senoritas.

The Indians walk over to the fire. They speak
in Dakota through Raven Feathers.

RAVEN FEATHERS

Painted Horse will lead you to the vanishing door.
The rest of the Sioux will leave to find the other braves.
Their spirits call to us. We will be with you later.

John and Tim walk over.

JOHN MACROY

What are the Sioux saying?

BIG BEN

Da' two of dem were just tellin' us why they's
leavin'. But they be comin' back.

JOHN MACROY

What's wrong Blue Wolf?

Blue Wolf

He responds. Raven Feathers interprets. I have a heavy spirit
for our two Sioux brothers who left to take meat to our
village. Something bad has happened. We must find them.

JOHN MACROY

I feel for you, my friend. Can someone join you?

Blue Wolf

Raven Feathers interprets- No, kindman. We will look and
join you later. I leave Painted Horse to guide the way.

JOHN MACROY

We will be thinking good thoughts and prayers for you.

They mount their horses. Blue Wolf and Raven Feathers depart.

BIG BEN

What jus' happened Sah?

JOHN MACROY

I don't know...just yet.

TIM MACROY

Dad, it's something he senses inside. I believe him.

ROD MCCULLA

Aboriginals consult the spirits and they know
what gives by cracky. I'd bet on it!

PONCHO GARCIA

Mi Madre, I mean my mother, she could read the tea leaves in
her cup and tell you what kind of a day you were going to have!

COOKIE

That's not right for you. It's her cup... it's her fortune.

PONCHO GARCIA

Aye Carumba. She kept telling me I needed to bring more
money to her to ward off my bad luck. The bad luck was hers.

ONE HOUR LATER

BIG BEN

So, I think I'll save my money and buy me some
horses and cows to start me a ranch.

Painted horse moves outside the campfire into the
darkness. He is spooked. He shouts out!

PAINTED HORSE

Wachita! Wachita! (White enemy! White enemy!)

He finds a place to hide in the night. The sound
of horse hoofs can be heard closing in.

JOHN MACROY

Quick men! ... Man, your weapons!

Everyone scrambles for Winchesters, pistols and Dino-rifles.

JOHN MACROY

I'll stay by the fire. Everyone spread out. Hide in the bushes
that circle the camp without shooting one another.

The horses' hooves are noisy. Finally, the fire reflects U.S.
Army on their military issued wagon and arms. The black
horses and blue uniforms dance in the fire's light.

MAJOR WILLS

There's the man! John MacRoy!

JOHN MACROY

Welcome Judas, I mean Major Wills. You
come in friendship I presume.

MAJOR COLE

Mr. MacRoy, I' m Major Cole. We understand
from Major Wills that you' re giving guns to the
Sioux and cavorting with illegal foreigners.

JOHN MACROY

The Indians are just hunting buffalo and have earned
anything I've given them. Should be no concern of yours.

MAJOR COLE

Oh...I think it's a great concern. We stopped two Sioux
dragging buffalo meat about 40 miles back and they
refused to relinquish their rifles and were shot!

JOHN MACROY

You Bastards!

The whole US Army squad points weapons at John.

JOHN MACROY

They were just takin' food home to feed their starving village.

MAJOR WILLS

No problem any more…We rounded up that village on the
Cheyenne (river) and put them in a stockade on the reservation.

MAJOR COLE

We' re told that you have Indians with you that
have rifles. We'd like to see them.

JOHN MACROY

Unfortunately Major, they left in a hurry.
I'm surprised you didn't kill them.

MAJOR COLE

First squadron…bear arms. Take aim!

They pull rifles and pistols and point them at John.

JOHN MACROY

I think we have you out flanked with impressive fire
power Major. Ben! Rod! Poncho! Tim! , Hans!

They all come closer to the fire to show the squad that
they 're surrounded with superior fire power.

JOHN MACROY

Now Majors, these here big guns you see several of
my men holding, were designed by Dr. Gatling for
me to bring down big game with rapid fire. I don't
think you'd like a demonstration laddies.

BIG BEN

It cuts da' trees down like wheat in a sickle.

JOHN MACROY

Your horse and you would be a pile of flesh.

MAJOR COLE

You're threatening the US Government Mr. MacRoy.

JOHN MACROY

No, I was warmin' up to a fire before you gentlemen came
upon me. I wasn't making any demands at the time.

MAJOR WILLS

Major Cole, He's got us out gunned. I've seen those big guns
demonstrated. They 're tornadoes fired out of a rifle.

MAJOR COLE

MacRoy your days are numbered. It's against the law
to arm the Sioux or any other Indian tribe.

JOHN MACROY

But not against the Law to kill innocent buffalo hunters
trying to feed their village? Instead, you put them on
reservations and give them powdered milk and rotten flour.

TIM MACROY

And the Army steals their blankets for
themselves. The fur traders told me.

MAJOR COLE

I' m just doing what the government pays me to do.

JOHN MACROY

Aye... if it were your family you 'd be singing a different
tune. Now, get the hell out of here. Put those shooters
away before we give in to an itchy trigger finger.

MAJOR COLE

OK men. Holster weapons on two. One!
Two! This isn't the end MacRoy!

JOHN MACROY

Oh, I'm sure of that. Next time we shoot
first, and ask questions later.
The Army Squadron travel out of sight. Reflections of
rising dust in the moonlight marks their departure.

JOHN MACROY

Let's get some sleep gents.

TIM MACROY

Dad, I feel very sleepy . I'm tired from all the hunting
of buffalo, butchering the ones we shot then traveling
back here and eating buffalo. I'm bushed.!

Tim goes into the covered wagon, lays down and falls asleep.
He dreams of a passage near the exit to 1881. Blue Wolf was
riding a large "T" Rex with a chief's head feathers and his
Winchester rifle. Rod McCulla was also riding a "T" Rex with
his Winchester rifle outstretched. Every cowboy and soldier
was firing at dinosaurs. Stange looking eagles flew overhead.

JOHN MACROY

Tim! Wake up. You're having a bad dream.

TIM MACROY

Dad, how long was I dreaming?

JOHN MACROY

About 2 hours

TIM MACROY

I'm wide awake now. I'll relieve Rod and finish first watch

JOHN MACROY

Ok, Tim..

JOHN MACROY (continued)

Hans.

HANS BECKER

Yes Mr. MacRoy.

JOHN MACROY

You 'll take Ben's watch at midnight.

HANS BECKER

Yes, sir.

JOHN MACROY

Take your Winchester rifles on watch.

The campfire continues to burn. Ben gets coffee
and gets ready to head to his post.

BEN

I want a cup of this black magic to keep me up.

TIM MACROY

I got some jerky. You want some Ben?

Cookie walks over.

COOKIE

I got jerky and hard-boiled eggs for both you. Taste
good, keeps you up, but you pass much wind. It's
OK, just stay away from my wagon. Thanks.

OTHER COWBOYS

Ha, ha, ha, ha, ha.

JOHN MACROY

...And stay away from the fire Laddies! Ha, ha, ha.

FOUR HOURS LATER

A sound of horses can be heard in the distance.

BIG BEN

Hey Mister Tim... Someone 's comin'.

He shouts to the camp.

BIG BEN

(cont)

Someone's comin'! WAKE UP EVERYONE!

Tim runs to see. Tuffy follows with one lonely Bark!

TIM

Look! It's Blue Wolf, Raven Feathers and
other braves. One looks wounded.

The camp wakes up and rustles about. Painted Horse
comes out of nowhere and greets his red brothers.

JOHN MACROY

What seems to be going on Lad?

TIM MACROY

Look! It' s Blue Wolf and the others.
Tuffy goes over and licks one of the wounded Indian
buffalo hunters as he gets down from his horse.

BIG BEN

And the one is hurt alright...Hey! He' s part of
da' buffalo hunters that left us early.

TIM MACROY

Tuffy come here boy.

Tuffy comes to Tim's side and lies down.

JOHN MACROY

Cookie, get the medicine box out.

COOKIE

I go now and get in big hurry.

He leaves for the wagon.

JOHN MACROY

How did he get shot?

RAVEN FEATHERS

His name is Fish Eagle and he said the Blue Coats
came from the South and overtook them.

JOHN MACROY

But why did they shoot them?

Raven Feathers questions wounded Fish Eagle in Dakota tongue.

RAVEN FEATHERS

The soldiers screamed for them to give up their rifles.
When they dropped them, then Blue Coats shot them.

JOHN MACROY

Those bloody bastards!!! Fish Eagle speaks up to Raven Feathers.

FISH EAGLE

We both were fired upon. I was lucky to have a fast
horse. My brother Owl Eyes died before me.

JOHN MACROY

Where did the other brave come from?

RAVEN FEATHERS

Talking Bird rode away when the Blue Coats attacked the village.

FLASHBACK

An army company of men charges a trusting, poorly
guarded Sioux village. People scatter, grab babies, flee
to the woods, screaming, crying and cursing. "Talking
Bird" rides away on his fast stead. Others were shot. The
remaining Sioux were forced to march to the stockade.

RAVEN FEATHERS

He crossed the plains where he saw Blue Wolf, myself,
and Fish Eagle. Talking Bird" is with us.

JOHN MACROY

Bloody Good! I hope we can help your cause. You
will always be our friends. Right boys?!

EVERYONE

Yes! You bet! I'm in! Me too! Count me in!

JOHN MACROY

All right then gents, we' re headed to a place beyond imagination.
Your life is depending on our knowledge to survive.

Ben is dressing Fish Eagle's wounds.

BIG BEN

Look Mista' Mac! Fish eagle's shot went clear through his
leg and one through his shoulder. He should be OK.

TIM MACROY

Here's alcohol. It will disinfect the wounds; then wrap it.

BIG BEN

I hear ya'

He closes and wraps it.

JOHN MACROY

Men, listen up! We're gonna' have to stay together.
Watch your backs. The Army's not our friend.

ROD MCCULLA

I think they've made that loud and clear.

JOHN MACROY

I'm uppin' the ante gents. I will pay $750 per
man when we find Virginia and return.

EVERYONE

Alright! I'm in! That's alot of green! Hooray! Hooray!

HANS BECKER

That is over seven months wages!

JOHN MACROY

We're packin 'up and headin' out. Raven Feathers,
could you have the braves lead the way.

BIG BEN

Boss, we should put "Fish Eagle" in the wagon 'til he's betta'.

JOHN MACROY

Then do it!

RAVEN FEATHERS

We will lead, Great One.

Raven Feathers talks Dakota tongue to the braves. Everyone
is mounted and riding horseback or in wagons.

ROD MCCULLA

I' d bet it' s not the last time we see our Army friends.

PONCHO GARCIA

In Mexico we can set our clocks for when the
Federally soldiers return to harass us.

HANS BECKER

I don't like killing, but when necessary. All the
guns are oiled, serviced and ready to go.

JOHN MACROY

Thanks Hans. We' ll need them directly, for sure.

BIG BEN

I'm confessin' to you, I hate 'dat Major Wills.
He's a bad man headed for HELL!

ROD MCCULLA

Eh Mate, he' s just a big looza'. (loser)

BIG BEN

What' s goin' on?

TIM MACROY

I am going up there to find out!

BIG BEN

Me too!
They meet the lead Indians. Their faces covered in grief
and bewilderment. It's a massacre of Kiowa Indians.
There is about thirty of them. All kinds are dead, that
includes women, children, elderly and a few braves.

BIG BEN (CONT)

It's Kiowa. Dey've been shot and it looks like they were unarmed.

John, Rod, Poncho, Cookie and Hans arrive.

JOHN MACROY

My Lord...They've been slaughtered. No enemy is dead with them.

PANCHO GARCIA

Mira (look) No one died with a weapon.

Rod reaches down and picks up large brass 50 caliber shell casings.

ROD MCCULLA

These are from the nasty weapon that took these natives down.

JOHN MACROY

Can I see one of those casings?

He reaches and retrieves one from Rod.

JOHN MACROY

Just as I thought. It's Army issue Gatling Gun 50
caliber rounds shot from ten rotating barrels. A large
mounted gun on canon style tow mount.

TIM MACROY

Dad. I read about how the Army slaughtered many Sioux
in the dead of winter at Wounded Knee. I heard THEY
DID IT to get back at the Sioux for "Little Bighorn"

JOHN MACROY

And I know What you' re going to say, they drove
them like sheep to a slaughter in Gatling Gun cross
fire. Killed the lot of them. No survivors!

ROD MCCULLA

Mista' Mac, I' d say that history' s repeated itself.

The Sioux search through the bodies for clues.

PAINTED HORSE

(Dakota Tongue)

I found something!

He picks up a bloody knife from a brave's grasping hand.

PONCHO GARCIA

May I see senor.

Painted Horse gives him the knife.

PONCHO GARCIA

Look at the tip, how it broke off showing fresh metal.
This Indian left it in someone›s bone. I would say his leg.
Aye Chihuahua, that is a man in a lot of pain.

JOHN MACROY

And it' s Army related.

RAVEN FEATHERS

MacRoy, The Kiowa are friends of the Sioux. We must
prepare their bodies for the Spirit World before we leave.

JOHN MACROY

And we will help. Gents pull the wagons up here
for a spell. We are going to help our Indian friends
set up a burial platform on cut branches.

RAVEN FEATHERS

We will help you cover the faces and put the bodies on the branches.

Everyone got the message. The corpses will be left
to be eaten by vultures, wolves and coyotes.

ROD MCCULLA

It's a damned shame the Army hates the natives.
In Australia the aboriginals show us the land and
how to live on it. A damned shame mates!

PONCHO GARCIA

In Mexico, we marry the natives... then we are them.

JOHN MACROY

OK Gents! Let' s get back on the trail.

Raven Feathers comes to John.

RAVEN FEATHERS

It' s complete. We put the wrapped dead Kiowa on burial stands.

JOHN MACROY

Raven Feathers, would you ask Painted Horse how far
away we are from the entrance to the dinosaur world?

He leaves and talks to Painted Horse then returns.

RAVEN FEATHERS

We must cross the Cheyenne River and ride into the plains above.

JOHN MACROY
I do remember now. That is an hour from here. Thanks.

TIM MACROY

What's next Dad?

JOHN MACROY

Laddie we're headed in to find Virginia.

TIM MACROY

Dad, it's almost a year since we left. Do you think she's...

JOHN MACROY

I don't know... but by the grace of God we're going to bloody
try. (Shouts)- OK Mates, let's load 'em up and head 'em out.

ONE HOUR LATER

EXTERIOR CHEYENNE RIVER -DAY

They drive the horses and wagons across the river.

PAINTED HORSE

(in Dakota)

It's up there on the plains below the hills where
menetonka (buffalo) once were.

JOHN MACROY

OK gents...head your horses toward those hills. The entrance
is there. It shimmers like heat rising in the desert.

ROD MCCULLA

Mr. Mac'...Look!

They view the river one thousand feet below to see about twenty-five U.S. Calvary soldiers crossing the Cheyenne (river).
JOHN MACROY

Tim, give me that telescope in the saddle. Thanks.

John focuses the magnification.

JOHN MACROY

(cont)

Yes, it's our friends in the U.S. Calvary. And there is the trouble maker, ex- Major Wills.

BIG BEN

Can I see Mr. Mac?

He hands Ben the telescope.

BIG BEN

It's 'dem alright and oh, Dat's bad. Look Mr. Mac'.

He hands the telescope to MacRoy.

BIG BEN

See that Gatling gun mounted like a canon.

JOHN MACROY

That wee piece of fire power is being set up to blast us!!!

The Indians are about one hundred yards ahead screaming to come. Raven Feathers rides back to John.

RAVEN FEATHERS

We have found the passage. Come!

JOHN MACROY

Put a step on its men! The passage is open ahead
and we're about to be fired upon.

Rat!Tat!Tat!Tat!Tat!Tat!...Pow! Pinc! Tink! Bam! Bam! Crash!
Zing! Zing! Bullets hit all around them. They ride hard as
the wagons sway and bounce. Ping! Ping! Two holes are left
in the wagon's canvas as the bullets fly. Tuffy growls then
lets out one bark and finds a blanket to hide under.

TUFFY

Grrrrr! Arf!

INSIDE THE WAGON

Cookie puts his finger through the bullet holes.

COOKIE

That's too close! It makes air for hot days. Ha, Ha, Ha.

TIM MACROY

You're funny, Cookie, but I hope we make it.

FROM THE ARMY UNIT IN THE DISTANCE- DAY

MAJOR COLE (shouts)

Stop in the name of the United States Army!

Blam! Pop! Blam! Pop! Pop!

JOHN MACROY

Sorry! We can't hear you.... Major Cole.

Blam! Blam! Blam! The riders and wagons make it through.

EXTERIOR CRETACIOUS PERIOD (100) MILLION
YEARS AGO-SOUTH DAKOTA-DAY

They all gather near the arrow tree. Here Blue Wolf shot an arrow
high in a fern tree to know where this vanishing entrance was.

JOHN MACROY

We all made it, thank God!

BIG BEN

Mister Mac", I say we go back by the stream where we last saw
Miss Deven. We can hide out in the trees and maybe see her.

JOHN MACROY

We need to get a move on it gents, let's go!!!

They travel quickly. Rooaar! A "T" Rex in the
distance let's everyone know who's boss. Small bat-
like lizards fly in swarms out of the trees.

FIFTEEN MINUTES LATER

Major Cole, Major Wills, and nine enlisted men make
it in with the wagon full of supplies towing the Gatling
Gun. An injured soldier rides in the covered wagon. He's
nursing an ankle wound from an Indian's knife.

MAJOR COLE

Sgt. Cribbs, take a look which way do you
think we should go to find MacRoy?

AAAAAAAAHHHHHHH! Smash! splat! The Army
mounted soldier and horse were cut in half. The
passage closed like a guillotine slicing the rider and
horse. They both whine for a brief moment.

PRIVATE SMITH

Oh My God! Have Mercy on his soul!

MAJOR COLE

It doesn't look like anyone else made it in after that. About twelve men left on the side we came from. It' s just us who made it in!

RRROOAARRR! a "T" Rex smells the blood and heads for a free meal. He' s determined to eat half horse and rider.
MAJOR COLE

Quickly men set up the Gatling Gun!!!

They quickly jump to it. It' s disconnected from the wagon and swung around just in time for a bandolier of bullets to be locked and loaded just in time.

PRIVATE RIGGS

Ready to fire!

MAJOR COLE

On my command...

The "T" Rex charges with its head low to the ground. RRROOAARR!!!

MAJOR COLE

(cont)

Fire!!!

POW! POW! POW! POW! POW! POW! POP! POP! POP! POP! POP! FLESH IS POPPING AND THE GIANT DINO KNEELS AND SPINS AROUND AND FALLS.

MAJOR COLE

Hold your fire! Hold your fire!

The dying Dino lays in a huge pool of his own blood. He chomps his jaws in a clicking reaction before death. The US Army realizes we are masters of this universe until the ammo runs out.

MAJOR WILLS

Did anyone see what direction MacRoy's crew went?

PRIVATE RIGGS

I thought that they went to the left, but I'm not sure.

MAJOR COLE

Fifth platoon prepare to travel up the plains to the left of
these trees. They can 't travel fast with those wagons.

They head out to the left of the jungle. Fear was forming
in their hearts with every noise and smell of this strange
land. The perspiration was not from the humidity.

SGT. CONNORS

There's somethin' ahead sir. Looks like horses.

They start to overtake them. They see that they're not horses...
but duck-billed dinosaurs, moving in a herd like horses do.

MAJOR WILLS

Would you look at that. That fox MacRoy was setting us up
all along. We save Virginia his fiancee, get killed by Prehistoric
beasts and he returns scott free. Doesn't even have to pay us!

MAJOR COLE

I'd agree if all we saw were the first type of predator, we killed...
but these seem pretty docile and look, they're vegetarians.

Some of the duck-billed dinosaurs stop to eat grass.

PRIVATE SMITH

Major, do you think we should take account of
who's here, so we know our force to the man.

MAJOR COLE

Great thinking private. Let's stop and go from rider to
rider. State your name, rank and serial numbers.
Major Wills reaches to give Private Smith
lined paper pad and pencil.

MAJOR WILLS

Private, take this and list all Army men of the Fifth Platoon.

MAJOR COLE

Major Wills who in God's name gave you
the authority to order around the
remainder of my Fifth Platoon?

MAJOR WILLS

Listen Major Coles we have limited time to stop MacRoy
from raising up the injuns to wipe us out, I tell ya'!

MAJOR COLE

I don't care what your time line is. You are not
to order any of my men around. You have no
authority. You are not on active duty. Got it!

MAJOR WILLS

Loud and clear, but I brought you here to stop
MacRoy from using Indians and foreigners to defeat
us. We are the United States of America!

MAJOR COLE

Now if you will excuse me Major Wills, I need to take role
here with Private Smith. Everyone gathers over here near the
wagon. We are taking roll call. When you hear PFC Cummings
call your name and rank say here and raise your hand...

PFC CUMMINGS

(Listen up.

1. Pfc James Johnson - here
2. Private Peter Zawaski - here
3. Private Markus Smith - here
4. Private Johnny Riggs - here
5. Private Meyer-ankle hurt - here
6. Private Mark Cripps - here
7. SGT. Connors - here
8. PFC Farmer - here
9. Major Claudius Cole - here
10. (myself) PFC Michael Cummings - here
11. Major Wills - here

PFC MICHAEL CUMMINGS

That makes eleven of us Major Cole. Private Meyer rubs
his wound with whiskey inside the covered wagon.

PRIVATE MEYER

OHH! Man does this wound hurt! Can someone
help me!? Damn Ankle! ow!ow!OWWWW!

Major Wills rides over to the covered wagon to see Private Meyer.

MAJOR WILLS

Listen Private Meyer if you don't quit your belly aching, I'm
gonna' have to shoot you like a wounded horse. Now shut up!

Private Meyers stops and moans quietly.

MAJOR COLE

Alright 1st Platoon listen up! We are separated from the rest of our
platoon. Private White died trying to pass into this hell hole. Our
goal is to find MacRoy & crew and bring them back dead or alive.

MAJOR WILLS

I like the "dead" part myself.

MAJOR COLE

(looking at Major Wills)

As I've stated before, all orders will come
from me only. Is that clear troops?
TROOPS

Yes, sir Major Cole!

MAJOR COLE
You two men on Horseback (Private Smith & Private Riggs)

SMITH & RIGGS

Yes Sir, Major Cole.

MAJOR COLE

Men I'm sending you to the place where we came
in this place. You will scout the plains on the right
of the trees for MacRoy and his crew.

PRIVATE SMITH & RIGGS

Yes sir!

PRIVATE SMITH

Major, we might only have about 3 hours of daylight left.

MAJOR COLE

Do you have a blanket, food rations and water?

PRIVATE SMITH & RIGGS

Yes sir!

MAJOR COLE

Ok, then you are seasoned U.S. Army soldiers. Report back
to me when you have any important information that will
help get MacRoy's group arrested. Do you understand?

PRIVATE SMITH & RIGGS

Yes Sir!

The two Privates mount their horses and proceed to
the entrance, Major Cole calls to Major Wills.

MAJOR COLE

Major Wills, could you please come with me. Let's see
how Private Meyer's doing with his leg being stabbed.

MAJOR WILLS

Sure. What a crybaby!

Majors Cole and Wills ride to the covered wagon. They dismount
and enter from the rear. Private Meyer is laying on a cot.

PRIVATE MEYER

Major Cole, ow! ouch!oh! This is killing me.

MAJOR WILLS

Well, we can speed up that process for you!

MAJOR COLE

Major Wills I would appreciate if I handle this...

Bang!Bang!Bang! Major Coles drops to the floor
dead! Shot by Major Wills' Colt 45!

MAJOR WILLS

I told you to follow my lead.

PRIVATE MEYER

You didn't have to kill Major Cole!

MAJOR WILLS

Your right, Bam! Bam! Bam!

Pvt. Meyer dies. Major Wills puts his Colt45
in Pvt. Meyer's right hand. Pvt Cripps and Sgt.
Connors arrive. They call in to Major Wills.

SGT. CONNORS

What's happened?

He asks as he walks into this bloody mess.

MAJOR WILLS

That bastard Private Meyers shot Major Coles just
because Major Coles told him to stop crying over a
minor injury. Coles wanted him to get back on his
horse and help us find MacRoy and his bunch.

SGT. CONNORS

So, what happened next?

MAJOR WILLS

Meyers shot Major Cole with one of my Colt 45s he pulled
from my holster. He didn't know that I was wearing two 45's.
I shot him 3 times with my other revolver. Let's bury these
two before the dinosaurs smell the blood. We need to fortify
our camp. Tomorrow we'll ride to arrest MacRoy's Camp.

SGT. CONNORS

I hate to bury two good soldiers in this prehistoric
jungle. Their families will morn without a burial.

MAJOR WILLS

Well, that may be so, but we must make the best
of this, so that we can arrest MacRoy's camp
tomorrow. Let's get out of this prehistoric Zoo.

SGT. CONNORS

Ok. Private Cripps let's get the rest of this Army to dig a double grave and we'll bring these bodies to have a burial the best that we can. Pvt Cripps Let's get a move on before dark.

PVT.CRIPPS

Yes sir. We'll start the digging directly.

Private Cripps and Private Zawaski get shovels and make burial plots for Major Cole and Private Meyer. They put make shift crosses at the head of the plots.

SGT.CONNORS

Major Wills could you help to wrap the bodies in Army issue blankets for the burial?

MAJOR WILLS

Yes, but let's hurry. Time's a wastin'.

Major Wills and Sgt. Connors bring the bodies to their marked graves, then put them in.

PVT. CRIPPS

Major Wills, we'll put dirt over the bodies and Sgt. Connors said he'd say a prayer.

MAJOR WILLS

Please do it quickly. I want you men to get ready to move and find MacRoy's camp in the morning.

SGT.CONNORS

It will be done sir. (Everyone bows your heads.) Dear Lord, please Bless Major Cole and PVT. Meyer as we lay them down to wait for heaven. Bless their families and loved ones we pray in Jesus' name. Amen!

Private Zawaski and Pvt.Cripps let me walk you to your lookout
positions. PFC. Cummings and PFC. Farmer join us to see your
lookout point you will be replacing in night watch 12:00 midnight.
The lookouts follow Sgt.Connors to their lookout posts

SGT. CONNORS

Before I give you orders to man your posts, I want
to tell you Major Wills is rotten to the core.

PVT. ZAWASKI

What do you mean?

SGT. CONNORS

I helped to clean up the dead bodies of Major Cole and Pvt. Meyer.
Major Wills told me that Pvt. Meyer stole his Colt45 from his
holster and shot Major Cole 3 times. Wills then said he shot Meyer
with his other colt 45, 3 times. Meyer laid dead with a colt 45 in
his right hand. Meyer was left- handed. Somehow, he also shot 3
bullets. I saw all 6 bullets gone from Meyers colt 45. I want all of you
to watch your backs when dealing with Major Wills. I'll talk more
about this later. Now let's get back to standing watch. I am putting
first watch post to Pvt Cripps in front of the large fern about 100
feet in front of our encampment. Let's all walk to the other post#2.

They all walk to lookout post #2

SGT.CONNORS

Pvt. Cripps will be replaced by Pfc. Cummings at 12:00
midnight until sunrise. Now see that large tree about 100
ft behind our encampment, they walk to the spot together.
Pvt. Zawaski you will do first watch 'till 12:00 midnight
Pfc cummings you will replace Zawaski at midnight and
watch 'till sunrise. I'm returning to camp. Keep what I told
you to yourselves, Major Wills is a killer and crazy man.

PREHISTORIC PLAINS AND JUNGLE SUNSET-NIGHTFALL

PRIVATE SMITH

Did you hear those gunshots? Three to begin with
and about 20 seconds later three more shots. What in
the Hell have we gotten ourselves into Riggs?

PRIVATE RIGGS

Yeah, it sounded like it came from our camp. What the hell are
they shootin' up? The first trouble with gunfire I'll never forget,
is when we came upon those Kiowa crossing the plains. I thought
we were in deep trouble when we approached all those Kiowa.

PRIVATE SMITH

They just stood there begging for mercy. The Majors pulled
the gatling gun out, and it was all over. It was a massacre.
Private Meyer walked through the dead bodies and was
stabbed in the ankle by a wounded Kiowa. He thought
he could take a knife from that not so dead Indian.

PRIVATE RIGGS

They didn't stand a chance. Now what in God's name is going
to happen to MacRoy's group when we report where they are?

PRIVATE SMITH

That sure gives us something to think about. We
could be kicked out of the Army and thrown in the
brig, if we don't follow Major Cole's orders.

PRIVATE RIGGS

It's something to think about alright. I guess the
Kiowa weren't blood thirsty that day.

They get to the end of the forest and turn their horses to the
right and proceed across the open plain. A large pterodactyl with
36-foot wingspan screeches above and spots them. The creature
swings around and dives in attack of the men and the horses.

PRIVATE SMITH

Hey! What's that?!

PRIVATE RIGGS

I don't know but let's ride for those trees RIGHT NOW!!

They pulled their horses into a fast gallop. Just as they made the outskirts of the forest, Private Riggs turns around to see this flying Dino' on top of them. He opens fire with his pistol.

Bam!Bam!Bam! The Pterodactyl pierces his horse' rear leg. It falls with rider. The flying dino' flaps its wings hoovering over the men. Bam!Bam!Bam!Bam! The pterodactyl pierces his horse's rear leg. It falls with the rider. The flying dino' flaps its wings hoovering over the men. They continue firing. BAM! BAM! BAM! BAM! They continue firing.

PRIVATE SMITH

Get over here Riggsy! Leave your horse for now.

He runs to Private Smith behind a large Fern tree.

PRIVATE RIGGS

Shoot that flyin' devil monster! Bam!Bam!Bam!
It doesn't bother him.

PRIVATE SMITH

Here (He Throws his rifle to Riggs) Shoot that overgrown Buzzard!

POW! POW! POW! POW!

PRIVATE RIGGS

Aim for his head. I'm shooting there with ya'!

Bam!Bam!POW!POW! Bam!POW!POW!

PRIVATE SMITH

LOOK he's falling out of the sky!

PRIVATE RIGGS

Let's finish him off!

PREHISTORIC PLAINS NEAR MACROY'S CAMP-DAY

JOHN MACROY

What in God's good name is goin' on over their mates?!

He points across the plain about a mile away.

BIG BEN

Mista' MacRoy I think they be Army scouts looking
fo' us. I don't think they be up to nothin' good.

TIM MACROY

They just got introduced to the land of the Prehistoric.
Welcome Dinosaurs. They hear the Army scouts shooting.

Blam! Bam! Bam! Minutes of silence follow.

ROD MCCULLA

Whatever creature it was it must be dead now. I think if these
are Army scouts, we better make camp in this horseshoe
shaped tree enclosure so nobody sneaks up on us mates.

JOHN MACROY

I first heard 6 shots far from us, Then multiple shots about a mile
across the way. Maybe 15 to 20 shots. They were being attacked
I'll bet. That sun is goin' down mighty soon. Let's get camp
situated. Those men may be coming to visit us in the morning.

COOKIE

I make a quick snack of cookies and coffee for those who stay
up for a watching. Chop, chop. Fire will be a small one.

PREHISTORIC PLAINS & FORESTS-
TWO SOLDIERS -NIGHT FALL

PRIVATE RIGGS

That flyin' lizard from hell! I think he hurt my horse really bad.

Riggs walks over to his horse that's laying on the forest floor.
PRIVATE RIGGS

Blacky, you got hurt. (Horse lets out a hurting
cry) I know you're feelin' bad.

PRIVATE SMITH

Riggs you gotta put that animal out of its' misery.

PRIVATE RIGGS

I know, I know Smitty, but its damn hard.

PRIVATE SMITH

Get over here. This will take a second.

Private Smith lines his revolver to the horse's head and
squeezes the trigger. Bam! The horse dies instantly.

JOHN MACROY'S CAMP -NIGHT

ROD MCCULLA

That shot must have been to put something out of its
misery. Let's hope an animal and not a human being.

JOHN MACROY

Everyone gets situated for a gunfight tomorrow. Tim, you stand
watch by that Fern tree over there (he points) south part of camp.

TIM MACROY

I hear ya'.

Tim hustles to the spot.

JOHN MACROY

Ben, you take a big Gatling rifle & Bandolier and
station yourself in front of the Wagons

BIG BEN

I got it covered Mister MacRoy.

Ben moves behind a pile of rocks about
50 feet in front of the wagons.

JOHN MACROY

Hans you will take Tim's post at twelve midnight and Poncho you
will relieve Big Ben at midnight as well. Everyone stays alert!!

PREHISTORIC JUNGLE-SMITH &
RIGGS BEDDOWN-NIGHT

PRIVATE RIGGS

Hey, this looks like a nice protected area we can make a fire.

PRIVATE SMITH

I'm workin' on the camp right now. I got a bunch
of Army rations when we left the Majors.

PRIVATE RIGGS

I'm tastin' those rations right now. Get the coffee goin' on that fire
you're makin'. I'll get out the Army cans of rations for our snack.

PRIVATE SMITH

Let's get your gear and move down a spell away from your horse.
That dead horse is gonna draw other creatures out of this forest
to eat free meat. I don't wanna be part of the free meat offer.

PRIVATE RIGGS

It's tough for me to think about "Blackie"
as just being a pile of meat.

PRIVATE SMITH

Okay, I'm sorry. Let's find a place to camp and get a fire going. We
can eat some of the "C" rations I got before we left. Give me some
of that canned ham. You can have the peanut butter. I hate it.

PRIVATE RIGGS

I'll look for some wood to start a fire.

PRIVATE SMITH

Watch for those nasty lizards! Keep one
hand on your 45 at all times.

PRIVATE RIGGS

Okay. Be right back

PRIVATE SMITH

I'll get the bedding set for our sleeping bags.
Just hurry up with the fire wood.

MAJOR WILLS ARMY CAMP-NIGHT

SGT. CONNORS

Did you hear the gun shots about an hour ago? I wonder
if Smith and Riggs ran into some dinosaurs.

MAJOR WILLS

Maybe John Macroy bushwacked them? I wouldn't put it past him.

SGT. CONNORS

It's going to wait 'till morning. We should get some sleep.
Those of you standing watch, keep your eyes peeled.

MAJOR WILLS

You men on watch stay awake, our lives depend on it.

SGT. CONNORS

Major Wills let's turn in, tomorrow's a big day.
MACROY'S CAMP MORNING -SUNRISE

MacRoy walks over to Cookie who is putting
eggs and bacon on the grill.

JOHN MACROY

That sure smells good Cookie! Let's get everyone
fed, then we look for Virginia.

COOKIE

Cookie makes man feel good inside, then he can go
outside in jungle and feel good to shoot bad monsters. I
can cook lizards and make them taste like chicken.

JOHN MACROY

The bottom line in this adventure Cookie, is to find Virginia.

COOKIE

You're right Mr. MacRoy. I will do my best to have
our crew feel good inside to find Miss Virginia.

ROD MCCULLA

John a lot of gunfire last night. I heard 6 rounds about
ten or more miles from here then 15 to 20 rounds fired
from the jungle across the way a couple of miles.

JOHN MACROY

I want to be smart. The Army thugs are trying to blast us off
the face of the earth. I want to give a look see for Virginia.

ROD MCCULLA

How will you find her John it's been over a year?

JOHN MACROY

This stream here was where the professor shot me and
Virginia. We lay in the pouring rain. Someone saw a Jungle
man come and steal away Virginia and go deep into the
forest. A Robinson Crusoe of this side of the Jungle.

ROD MCCULLA

Well John I've been hunting in Jungles all
my life. Let me go with you.

TIM MACROY

I'd like to go too!

JOHN MACROY

Okay son I want just us three. Cookie, can you
make food sacks for us for a two-day trek?

COOKIE

I make good food and canteens of water.

JOHN MACROY

Ben, could you get one of those gatlin' rifles and 3-4 belts of ammo?

BIG BEN

I surely will Mr. MacRoy. Why don't I join you too?

JOHN MACROY

Ben, I need for you to make this a battle safe pavilion
for any attacks from the Army or dinos. If you see
Blue Wolf, send him in the jungle after us.

COOKIE

I Almost finish your food bags and water
canteens for you. You like very much!

JOHN MACROY

Everyone left behind come round: Big Ben, Hans Becker, Cookie,
and Poncho Garcia. Blue Wolf, Raven Feathers and the Rest
of our Indian friends send them to find us in the jungle when
they show up. Hold down our station here until we return.

PONCHO GARCIA

You don't worry, we will hold the camp down and make it mucho
deficil (really hard) for any intruders - Army or dinosaur.

JOHN MACROY

I hope to find Virginia soon. Stay alive for our return. $750
for each of you when we find Virginia and return home.

EVERYONE

Alright, yippee, real good!

ROD MCCULLA

John are we each taking a horse to pack out. One horse should
have a gatling rifle and another carry 3 bandoliers of bullets. A
Winchester Rifle for each man, along with several boxes of rounds.

JOHN MACROY

Sounds good. Do it;

TIM MACROY

Can I also wear my six shooters dad.

JOHN MACROY

Surely, you know how to use them. Time's a
wastin'. Let's get our stuff together and go!

JOHN MACROY AND CREW LEAVE
TO FIND VIRGINIA-MORNING

JOHN MACROY

Ben, Poncho, Hans, and Cookie, be sure you protect
our camp while we go look for Virginia

ROD MCCULLA
Take care for our return when we find her!

JOHN MACROY

Big Ben, you guys. think smart. We'll be back!

BIG BEN

Don't you worry Mr. MacRoy. We be holdin' down our forest camp!

MORNING SUNRISE – ARMY CAMP - 2 HOURS LATER
The Army's camp woke up. Coffee was made with some
biscuits, and "C" rations. Major Wills looked out in the
plains with his binoculars to see MacRoy's camp. He sees
and hears Pvt. Smith and Pvt. Riggs who were riding
double back on one horse toward the Army camp.

MAJOR WILLS

What are those idiots trying to do?! They are riding right near
MacRoy's camp. Pvt. Cripps, get me my horse and do it quickly!

Major Wills mounts his horse and makes sure he has his
rifle and 45 pistols in holster. He rides quickly to intercept
Pvt Riggs and Pvt. Smith. He is upon them in no time.

MAJOR WILLS

So, gentlemen, why did you not get set up to spy on
Macroy's camp as ordered by me?! We would be ready to
attack his camp right now. You men are worthless!

Major Wills pulled out his Winchester rifle. He started firing at them as they galloped away, both riding on one horse. BAM! BAM! BAM! The ground started shaking like an earthquake. Sgt. Connors was watching and feared Major Wills would kill them. He mounts his horse and PFC Farmer and PFC Cummings mount theirs and join him. They went after Major Wills. Sgt. Connors, PFC. Farmer and PFC Cummings ride to meet up with Crazy Major Wills.

MAJOR WILLS

Sgt. Connors, PFC. Farmer and PFC. Cummings, Why
do I have the pleasure of meeting you out here? You
men are just as worthless as Pvt. Smith and Pvt. Riggs!
I may as well shoot your asses while you're here.
The earth now started to quake violently. The T -Rex were
chasing a large herd of dinosaurs- triceratops, duckbilled dinos,
Stegosaurus and more. Major Wills shot his rifle up in the air.

He then was bucked off his horse as several dinos from this
stampede ran over him. He was able to slowly get to his feet
and stand upright. Suddenly, in a matter of seconds a "T" Rex
swallowed him head and upper body first then gulped him down.

SGT.CONNORS (Shouting over Dinosaurs)

Okay men. Beat it on back to our camp; Stay together!

Sgt Connors, Pfc. Cummings, and Pfc. Farmer ride quickly
through the stampeding dinosaurs toward the U.S. Army
Camp. Big Ben sees them knowing Major Wills was just
killed by the dinosaurs in stampede. Big Ben sees their
dilemma and waves them into Macroy's camp.

BIG BEN

You all come in here! Come on be safe!

They see Ben waving them in a side opening to the camp.

SGT. CONNORS

Whoa horses! Come in here! Good Boys!

All three horses and men make it in okay.
Poncho and Ben help them down.

PONCHO GARCIA

We are all glad you do not have to put up with Major
Wills. He was mui loco. I mean very crazy for sure.

BIG BEN

Let's get our guns over to the place you came in from.
We don't want a mean dino to come in. They are still
chasing their supper, and I don't want to be it!

Just then, two Raptors detour into camp. They let
out a terrible hissing sound and growl like a mean cat.
Everyone raises their rifles and aims at them.

SGT. CONNORS

Okay men! Ready, Aim! Fire! BAM! BAM!
BAM! BAM! BAM! POW! POW!

The Raptors tried to run at the men, but now Big
Ben has his Gatling Rifle and he's aiming at their legs.
POW! POW! POW! POW! POW! POW! POW! POW!
Both Raptors went down. It stopped in silence.

BIG BEN

Let's take our rifles and finish off the dying dinos. They
still have sharp teeth and claws to try and hurt us.

JOHN MACROY AND CREW HEAD EAST THROUGH
THE JUNGLE TO FIND VIRGINIA-MORNING

ROD MCCULLA

Let's head over there.

He points east toward short bushes. There appears to be a trail.

JOHN MACROY

That's great for the horses. Keep your eyes peeled
for any wild dinos with an attitude.

ROD MCCULLA

They're on my list of bad animals.

TIM MACROY

I'm lookin' too Dad.
John, Tim and Rod march on a small path with
their horses for about 1/2 an hour.

ROD MCCULLA

John, do you have a feeling?

JOHN MACROY

What? That we're being watched?

ROD MCCULLA

You in the tree! Come down before you get shot!

JUNGLE MAN

I'm just a lookout to protect my family. I'm coming down.

As he descends, a woman comes to him with a small
baby in arms. John and Tim look astonished.

JOHN MACROY

VIRGINIA!.IS THAT YOU?!!

VIRGINIA

Yes John, we both lived to see another day.

JOHN MACROY

Yes, my love, I've wagered my all to find you.

The baby starts to cry. waa, waa, waa!

ROD MCCULLA

We found Virginia!

VIRGINIA DEVEN

You have met my husband Dr. Bernard.
DR. ADAM BERNARD

John, I met you in the Jungle over a year ago. I heard
gunshots. I saw you and Virginia wounded lying next to the
creek in the pouring rain. You both were shot and bleeding
badly. I quickly put Virginia on a makeshift tree branch
sled and took her back to my house in the jungle.

JOHN MACROY

They dragged me out of the pouring rain and back into the
covered wagon. The villain of our group, Professor Perkins,
was the one who shot me and Virginia. I thought to myself,
we met our goals to find Virginia and met her husband, Dr.
Bernard and baby- Ginny . We just have to find a way out of
this prehistoric zoo. The thought of home sounded so good!

VIRGINIA

The baby's name is Virginia also but we just call her Ginny. She
is so much fun in this humid danger-filled jungle. Come inside
our modest jungle villa. We have coffee or tea to offer you.

They go inside and sit at homemade table and chair set.
Rod and Tim took a cup of tea and John a cup of coffee.

VIRGINIA

Tim it's so nice to see you. Has your dad been
teaching you more about firearms?

Yes Miss Virginia, oh I mean Mrs. It is so good to see you. We
were worried that you might not have made it after you got shot.

VIRGINIA

Tim, I was bleeding to death in the pouring rain. Doctor
Bernard found me, and carried me back to this home.
He used his training and medicine to save my life.

DR. ADAM BERNARD

She had severe blood loss from 2 gunshots. She had one to
the edge of her liver and another in her thigh. This patient
healed fully. I bandaged her and put her on vitamins and
blood healers. Look here are the two slugs that I removed.

He dumps two crunched bullets on the wooden table. Kerplunk!

JOHN MACROY

Well doctor, how did you end up here in dinosaur land?

DR. ADAM BERNARD

Good question John. Six years ago, in 1875 my 1st wife, Caroline,
and I were crossing South Dakota traveling from Chicago, Illinois.
We met nice folks along the way who needed a doctor. I was to be
a resident doctor of Sioux Falls Hospital and work full time. We
were lost. Our horses pulled our wagon into a chasm that led to
100 million years ago. It appeared to be the Cretaceous Period.

JOHN MACROY

You had a similar experience as did our Indian friend Blue
Wolf. He was hunting buffalo in the Black Hills above
the Cherokee River when he was attacked by a Triceratops
dinosaur that charged him from a chasm straight out of
dinosaur land. It's this crazy place we're in right now!

DR. ADAM BERNARD

We traveled back in time, when dinosaurs roamed the
earth. T-Rex and Velociraptor were the bad lizards that
killed our horses and Caroline when I was hunting
for food. I lived by myself for the next six years.

ROD MCCULLA

So how did you find VIRGINIA?

DR. ADAM BERNARD

Twelve Months ago, I heard gun shots near the stream in the
open plain. I could see two people shot laying on the side of
the water. Someone came out of a covered wagon. He was
told to bring the two persons shot into the covered wagon.
He had a hard time carrying the large man into the wagon.
JOHN MACROY

That's because the large man was me!

DR. ADAM BERNARD

I dashed out to get Virginia. I carried her to my jungle home.
I turned my lantern on. I quickly stopped the bleeding. I
had the right bandages and Medicine. I took these two nasty
bullets from her thigh and liver. She had a small wound at
the bottom of the liver. The liver can regenerate and build
itself back to normal. I waited on her day and night.

VIRGINIA

We became inseparable. We do look forward to getting out of here.

JOHN MACROY

We can offer you protection to leave with us.

VIRGINIA

Thank you, John. You're an angel.

DR. ADAM BERNARD

That's a great offer John. We would love
to get out of this HELL HOLE!

ROD MCCULLA

I can hear gunshots in the distance!

Bam!Bam!Bam!.......silence........Bam!Bam!Bam!

JOHN MACROY

Doc put together your doctor kit. Virginia, quickly pack things
for you and the baby. WE NEED TO LEAVE NOW!!!
They threw together allot of baby things, food, clothing and guns.

VIRGINIA

We're ready! I have a papoose to carry lil' Ginny.

JOHN MACROY

Tim, you need to give your horse to Virginia for her and baby to
Travel. We are not traveling in a race. A fast walk will suffice Tim.

ROD MCCULLA

Doc packs your meds in my empty saddle bag.

JOHN MACROY

Let's get while the getting's good!

The five adults and one baby follow the jungle path
back to MacRoy's camp. They finally arrive after
about an hour of swift travel. He's surprised see
their camp had joined forces with the Army.

Big Ben

Well, look who's here! It's John, Rod, Tim and even Miss Virginia!

VIRGINIA

Ben this is my baby girl little Virginia. We call her Ginny.
This is her father and my husband, Dr. Adam Bernard.

JOHN MACROY

Excuse us Virginia,

Ben, what has happened since we've been gone?
I see the U.S. Army in our camp?

Sgt. Connors walks up to John.

SGT. CONNORS

Sir we have gone through Major Wills killing Major Cole, and Pvt.
Meyer. He attempted to gain control. He was the force trying to
kill you all and the Indians. He got his just ending. A giant "T"
Rex ate him while he attempted to shoot me and my two Privates.
I am now in charge and you are not our enemy. Major Wills was!

JOHN MACROY

Sgt. Connors, Thank you for your gentile spirit. We all
need to stick together if we're getting' out of this place.

Pvt Riggs and Pvt. Smith show up riding double back.

PVT. RIGGS

Howdy. We made it to a mixed camp.
MacRoy's men and the U.S. Army.

PVT. SMITH

Yes, we did, and Crazy Major Wills came out from camp
to try and shoot us. He couldn't shoot straight at me and
Riggsey cause a mean old dino ate him for breakfast.

PVT. RIGGS

I can remember it all like a bad dream gone well!

ROD MCCULLA

Now listen up! We've got to get organized to make a
break for that crazy opening and get back to 1881. Let's
get a march going toward the way out of here.

John and Rod talk to each other on horseback.

JOHN MACROY

Rod, the U.S. Army is ahead of us to be the first to exit at the arrow tree. I can't stop thinking about Blue Wolf, Raven Feathers and other Indians who vowed to come back. They left us to protect their people from the U.S. Army killing Indians.

ROD MCCULLA

So, the Indians could possibly show up during our exit, and the Army is leading the way. What can go wrong! (tongue in cheek)

JOHN MACROY

Everything!! We could have a major fight before we can exit.

ROD MCCULLA

I think we should discuss this with Sgt. Connors. We need to intermingle our people in between Army personnel. It would dissuade the Indians to shoot the Army men who helped us return to civilization.

JOHN MACROY

Rod, could you talk to Sgt Connors? Have him tell his troops to intermingle with the rest of our folks. Let's project a united peaceful group.

ROD MCCULLA

Good thinking. I'll talk with Sgt. Connors.

Rod goes to the front of the march formation to Sgt. Connors.

ROD MCCULLA

Sgt. Connors This is important. Could we stop the caravan going out of here? I would like to talk with all the Army men we have here today. Our lives depend on it!

SGT.CONNORS

Every enlisted man listens up. I need for all here today whether
on horseback, on foot or in our wagons to meet right here
for a talk. Move in close so you can hear Mr. McCulla

ROD MCCULLA

Hi, my name is Rod McCulla. I'm an Australian cowboy
working for John MacRoy. We all have gone through a lot in
our stay in this nightmare. Crazy Major Wills attacked our
family of adventurers including civilians, soldiers, people from
other countries and our American Indians. We civilians came
to search for Virginia Devens who was lost, wounded and left
here for dead about a year ago. Can you come here Virginia?

Virginia walks over to Rod with baby Ginny.

VIRGINIA

How can I help Rod?

ROD MCCULLA

Virginia, can you tell these men how you and husband
Dr. Bernard managed to live this past year here?

VIRGINIA

Fourteen months ago. I and John Macroy and a bunch of cowboys
searched for this prehistoric Place. We came to find Chief Red
Eagle's son, Blue Wolf. He chased a dinosaur through a time
chasm back 100 million years. John came here for some hunting
trophies but primarily to find "Blue Wolf". I and John were shot
by an escaped convict, Mr. Starks, who posed as a Paleontologist.
We were left for dead. That stream that we passed is where we
were left to die in the pouring rain. Dr. Bernard, who lived here
alone, came out of the jungle and took me to his homemade
cabin. There he operated on me and saved me. The only way to
survive here is a close bond to protect you from the many perils.

ROD MCCULLA

We need to stick together for what may be ahead We
may meet a hand full of friendly Indians on our way
out. No one is to shoot them or fight They will come
perhaps to help us go back to our world in 1881.

SGT. CONNORS

That's why we are to intermingle with John MacRoy's
group. Everyone hear me and understand?

ARMY MEN
We want to help! Yes sir! Loud & clear! We're with you!

FLASHBACK
SGT.CONNORS

I remember when we ran from the Dino stampede into
Macroy's camp. Crazy Major Wills was killed by being
trampled by the raging Dinosaurs and eaten by the T-Rex.

SGT CONNORS

We barely made it into Macroy's camp
thanks to Big Ben and his men.

FLASHBACK

BIG BEN

Hey men let them ride into our camp! Come
in here, come in here you'll be safe!

SGT. CONNORS

They're calling us into safety. Head into their camp men.

They veer off of the large treeless plain into MacRoy's camp.

Poncho and Big Ben Help them with their horses.

BIG BEN

Let's tie up your horses and get your rifles. We
got to keep on shooting. We don't want any of
those big ones coming in this tree area.

Everyone is behind a tree firing at the dinos.

BIG BEN

Sgt. Connors could you get your boys to come
over here and join us to fight these giants?

SGT. CONNORS

Thats a great idea mr________?

BIG BEN

Jus' call me Ben.
SGT. CONNORS

OK I'm headed out I'll try and get our big gun
to use on those giant lizards too.

He heads out carefully amidst the stampede. He weaves
in & out of the dinosaurs. Finally arrives with the rest
of his men in the Army camp across the way.

SGT. CONNORS

Get your gear together. We are joining MacRoy's
camp. Crazy man Major Wills tried to kill

Pvt. Smith and Pvt. Riggs. Then He tried to kill
myself and Pfc. Farmer and Pfc. Cummings.

We were worried about the stampede. We could hardly
see you and PFC Cummings and PFC. Farmer.

SGT.CONNORS

Major Wills had thousands of pounds of dinosaurs stomping on his
wicked ass and snacking on his rotten body. Gentlemen lets go over

to our friends at MacRoy's camp. Pfc. Cummings and Pfc. Farmer are already there shooting dinosaurs with MacRoy's group of guys.

SGT.CONNORS AND REMAINING SOLDIERS CROSS OVER TO MACROY'S CAMP

SGT. CONNORS

Men Watch your directions with this wagon pulled by the horses. Follow my lead Pvt Zawasky. Steer the horses in a straight shot for MacRoy's camp across the way. Pvt. Cripps and Pvt. Johnson bring up the rear behind the wagon. Is our Gatlin Gun still attached to the rear of the wagon?

PVT.JOHNSON

Yes. Sir we also have plenty of ammo in the wagon.

SGT. CONNORS

Men! Wagons and horses FORWARD!
The dinosaurs gallop around the Army formation. A loud shaking sound is slowly stopping. Rumble. Rumble. The dinos let out intermittent screams. Sgt. Connors rides into Macroy's camp.

BIG BEN

Ok you all, lets help Sgt. Connors and his men
get set up with that large Gatlin Gun.

The Army soldiers start moving the large Gatlin gun and secure a large ammo belt on it. Others help to set up a firing line against the Dinos. The dinosaurs in the plain have calmed down. The T-Rexes and Velociraptors are not chasing others for a meal. They appear to be about 1-5 miles out eating dead dino bodies.

John MacRoy and crew enter the camp. He is surprised how well the Army joined forces with MacRoy's camp.

JOHN MACROY

Ben, what has happened? The Army seems to be
working with us nicely. Let's get more organized
now and get out of this Dinosaur devil pit!

Sgt. Connors walks up to John.

SGT. CONNORS

John, I like the way you put that. We have gone through hell
since (retired) Major Wills took charge. He worked it so that
he shot and killed Major Cole. He blamed it on a wounded
Pvt. Meyer and shot and killed him. Major Cole before his
death sent Pvt Smith and Pvt. Riggs to scout your camp. They
were attacked by a flying dinosaur that killed Smitty's horse.

ROD MCCULLA

I remember hearing the shots fired across this plain.

SGT. CONNORS

Major Wills was upset to find out the scouts were unable to spy
on your camp. Wills rode out to shoot them. I didn't want Major
Wills to kill any more, so I quickly rode out to stop him with
two other Pfc's. He tried to shoot me, but a wild stampede of
dinosaurs saved our lives. They scared his horse; it reared up and
dropped Wills. He was trampled on. He tried to stand up, but a
large "T" Rex Stuffed him in his mouth and swallowed him. I am
now in charge, and you are not our enemy. Major Wills was.

ROD MCCULLA

I was hoping your presence didn't mean
we are heading for a stockade.

JOHN MACROY

Sgt. Connors, Let 's get situated. Thank you for your
gentile spirit and caring attitude. Rod, find Cookie
and have him make some food for all of us.

Cookie

You don't look very far for me. It's time to cook
too much for us and Army. Ha, Ha, Ha!

VIRGINIA

John can Cookie find something baby Ginny could eat?

COOKIE

I have some goat's milk and some cookies. It's
so good to see you again Miss Virginia.

VIRGINIA

Cookie I'm Mrs. Virginia Bernard now. Married
to the Doctor that saved my life.

Pvt. Smith and Pvt. Riggs come into common ground away from
the bloody plains. They shake hands with all to say they made it.

TIM MACROY

Hi Cookie what's for chow?

COOKIE

Young man, I got to set up fire for barbeque
meat. Big steaks taste really good!

TIM MACROY

I love barbeque steaks!

COOKIE

Now get help to make big wood fire so Cookie
can put two big kettles for steak and beans.

TIM MACROY

I'm going to get Poncho and Big Ben to Help!

Tim goes and rounds up Big Ben, Poncho, Hans Becker, and several Army guys who asked to help for supper. They Come back with bundles of wood including some stashed in their wagon.

COOKIE

Me very happy. I wish we can make three big
fires, but we only have two big kettles.

SGT. CONNORS

I overheard you, Cookie. We happen to have two
large Kettles in our wagon we can use.

PVT. CRIPPS

I have those kettles right here! Sorry Sargent Connors. I overheard.

COOKIE

Now set up four fires, with kettle hanger if you have. If not, we
put direct on coals. In about 30 minutes we put food on fires.
EVERYONE

Horray! Yippee! thanks Cookie!

TUFFY – BARK! BARK!

COOKIE

Okay Tuffy, Cookies saves nice bone with meat for you. Okay?!

TUFFY-Ruff! Ruff!
COOKIE -but no fortune cookie for you, Ha, Ha,

The pots boiled the meat with Chinese spices, potatoes,
carrots, garlic, rice. Chinese noodles and herbs.

JOHN MACROY

Ok men and Mr. and Mrs. Bernard let's give one
big applause to the success of our mission!

EVERYONE

Yipee! Horray! That's great!

JOHN MACROY

We found the long-lost Virginia with a nice surprise, she got
married to the Doctor Bernard and had a baby, little Ginny.

EVERYONE

Applause......clapping" Horray!"

Cookie walks over to John

COOKIE

People! Food is ready! Hans's ova dere and Pancho ova
dere; form two lines and get plates, forks and knives. They
will serve you with big spoons. Go now chop, chop!

ROD MCCULLA

People! Let's eat fast. We want to finish eating before
the dinosaurs start up again. We need to eat and pass
through the magic portal before it gets dark.

Everyone is eating and enjoying. It is one big family, Army included.

BIG BEN

Mr. MacRoy, what ever happened to Blue Wolf
and his braves. It's like they just' vanished.

JOHN MACROY

Ben, they kind of made themselves scarce when the Army
attacked Indians in general. I hope we see them again.

SGT. CONNORS

John I'm sending Pvt. Cripps to relieve Hans and Pvt. Smith
to relieve Pancho. Almost everyone has been fed. My men
will clean up bowls, plates, pots & pans after chow.

COOKIE

I'm so happy you make soldiers clean up everything.
Afta' such good meal all very happy, yes?!

JOHN MCROY

Everyone enjoyed your beef stew.

COOKIE

That not beef, I made it better than beef. I keep lots
of this meat for our meal. Cookie is best cook.

JOHN MACROY

Everyone gets ready to travel home. Pack up and get ready to go.

SGT. CONNORS

Listen up! If you are in the U.S. Army, Get packed up to
leave this God forsaken place and head for home.

VIRGINIA

Cookie! Cookie! Hi Cookie. Thank you for the goat's milk
and cookies for little Ginny. She rocks Ginny while she eats.

COOKIE

Lil' Ginny is pretty like momma. Like you! ha! ha! ha! I
very happy you are alright and got better with Doctor's
help. Now he's your husband. Right? Right!

VIRGINIA

Cookie you are the best!

COOKIE

When we get back to town, Cookie will find a place for
Chinese restaurant, find a wife, and make Chinese babies!

VIRGINIA

I'm sure you will Cookie. Ha, Ha! I'm sure you will!

ROD MCCULLA

Everyone who has a horse, pack him out with guns and ammo.
If you have no horse, you will be in the wagon or be walking!

BIG BEN

Look at the plains. Most of those dino lizards have left.
Slow March to the arrow tree so we can go back home. It's
about 1 mile ahead. LET'S GO YOU ALL, LET'S GO!!

EVERYONE -ARMY & CIVILIAN MARCH
TOWARD THE ARROW TREE -DAY

ROD MCCULLA

John, I have one of the Gatlin rifles ready to use, how
about the other two Gatlin rifles. Who's got them?

JOHN MACROY

The other two and ammo belts are in the wagon with Ben.

ROD MCCULLA

Ok I'll talk with Ben.
McCulla rides over to the wagon. Ben, Cookie, Virginia and
baby are in the wagon. Tim Macroy and Doctor Bernard
walk along side of wagon. Virginia talks to Dr. Bernard.

VIRGINIA

Sweetheart, could you go in the wagon and get my
bag of clean clothes that I use for diapers?

DR. BERNARD

You want that grey bag?

VIRGINIA

Yes, the one with your old undershirts that I use for diapers.

DR. BERNARD

Sure sweetheart, I'll be back in a moment.

He asks Pvt. Smith if he would help.

DR. BERNARD

Private could you give this bag of rags to my wife over there? She needs to change us Baby Ginny?

PVT. SMITH

I'd be happy to.

DR. BERNARD

Thank you.

DINOSAURS SPOOK HORSES, DR. BERNARD AND ROD GET INTO THE WAGON TO SAVE EVERYTHING- DAY

Horses scream and Dr. Bernard and Rod McCulla are up in the wagon to try and calm them. They pulled the wagon in the opposite direction, away from the exit. Dr. Bernard and Cookie both try to get the team of horses to calm down. Rod is standing up on one of the horses trying to pull the team over. The horses go crazy raising up and kicking a raptor.

ROD MCCULLA

Ok my little horsey friends. Listen to Rod. We need to turn around and go out of this place. Okay? Whoa! Whoa! It's okay my babies. Someone gets a rifle and shoot that mean dinosaur on my left.

COOKIE

I got rifle and wait for mean dino to move. Now move a little more BAM! BAM! BAM! BAM! Oh, look Rod, dino has a bad headache and fell on the ground to play dead. Ha! Ha! Ha! I don't think he's playing this time.

The horses hear Rod's kind voice and listen. The wagon turns around the right direction to 180 degrees. Rod meets back with Sgt. Connors.

ROD MCULLA

Now let's head out to the magic exit. We need to stick together for what may be ahead. We may meet a handful of friendly Indians on our way out. No one is to shoot them or fight. They will come perhaps to help us to go back to our world in 1881.

SGT. CONNORS

That's why we are to intermingle with John MacRoy' group. Everyone hear me and understand?

ARMY MEN

We want to help. Yes sir, loud and clear. We're with ya'.

SGT. CONNORS

Okay, let's go!

ROD MCCULLA

We need to stick together for what may be ahead. We may meet a handful of friendly Indians on our way out. No one is to shoot them or fight. They will come perhaps to help us to go back to our world in 1881.

SGT. CONNORS

That's why we are to intermingle with John MacRoy's group. Everyone hear me and understand?

ARMY MEN

We want to help. Yes sir, loud and clear. We're with ya'.

SGT. CONNORS

OK let's go!

Tim MacRoy jogs to the front of everyone and speaks.

TIM MACROY

I know where the magic arrow tree is! Last year I had
to shoot and kill a "T" Rex for us all to get out.

SOLDIERS

Alright way to go Tim!!!

SGT. CONNORS

Tim, stay up here with us in the lead so we can find
the Arrow Tree. Let's exit this terrible hole!

John MacRoy Walks over.

JOHN MACROY

You had a chance to meet my son, Tim. He's a good shot.
Mrs. Virgina taught him. She's the daughter of a famous
trick shot artist. Her mother was Annie Oakley. Tim still
wears his six shooters and holster belt. Virginia gave it to
him when she taught him how to be a trick shot artist.

Tim shows off his prize

So, laddies let's get a move on it. We'll intermingle with you gents
with guns ready. Don't shoot at any Indians. They're friends.

The mixed group headed toward the mysterious exit at the
arrow tree. They all looked perplexed. It felt like the rumbling
of an earthquake. They heard Shrieks and roars. They looked
up to see a dinosaur stampede heading toward them.

SGT. CONNORS

Quick, get the lead wagon and sharpshooters form a semi-circle in front of the hoard coming at us! Move the large Gatlin Gun pointing right at them! Aim it at the head of the Pack!

BAM! BAM! BAM! BAM! BAM! BAM! BAM1 Giant lizards were falling. Suddenly the large Gatlin gun jammed! Duckbilled dinos, Triceratops, Spinosaurus with large finned backs all being chased by several Tyrannosaurus Rex. Dinosaurs that had been shot were dropping everywhere.

The large Gatlin gun stopped firing. Rod McCulla and Big Ben were shooting at them with their Gatlin rifles. They were running low on ammo clips.

ROD MCCULLA

Hey Ben! I've only one ammo belt left. How about you.

BIG BEN

I have 1/2 of a belt left.

ROD MCCULLA

John! Can you check to see if we have any more gatling rifle ammo belts around.

JOHN MACROY

I'm afraid were down to the last we've got. The gun mechanics Are trying to get the Army's large gatling fixed. Everyone! Use your Winchester rifles when the Gatlings cease to fire.

PVT. JOHNSON

Look! Some Indians ON HORSEBACK have entered through the chasm near that arrow tree! Don't shoot those Indians on horseback! There are friends

JOHN MACROY

Blue Wolf!! Blue Wolf!!Come here! So good to see you!

Raven Feathers tells Blue Wolf in Sioux language.
Raven Feathers, please tell Blue Wolf to get the other
braves and shoot from here at the dinos.

ROD MCCULLA

Get READY! The dinos are heading for us. Let them have it!

Wam! Bam!Bam! BAM! BAM! WAM! BAM!.........

Blue Wolf and Raven Feathers ride over to talk to John,
while four other braves stay in position to shoot dinos.

JOHN MACROY

Blue Wolf, so good to see you! Get your other braves
and form a line of defense right here by the wagons.

Raven Feathers interprets and he and Blue
Wolf get his braves to come over.

JOHN MACROY

Ben, find everyone that has a Gatlin rifle to load up and come
here. We're ready for a dino charge in that grassy plain before us.

All fire power is aimed at the dinosaurs out
there 100 ft.to 200 ft in the plains.

ROD MCCULLA

Get ready men! The Dinos are headed for us! Rumble! Rumble!
Fire!!! BAM! BAM! BAM1 POW! POW! BAM! BAM! BAM!
SHOOTING GOES ON FOR 30 MINUTES STRAIGHT!
Approximately 50 dead dinosaurs fill the fields.

ROD MCCULLA

Look1 In the South of here. There's our
wagon going the wrong way!!

Rod gets on his horse. I'm headed out to turn that wagon around.

BLUE WOLF

(He speaks through Raven Feathers)
Stop firing at the dinosaurs. I Blue Wolf will go behind
the dinosaurs and draw them away while Rod goes to
get the run-away wagon. Everyone else. Go through
THE MAGIC PASSAGE WAY. I'll take all my braves
and fight those evil ones. Now let us go quickly.

JOHN MACROY

Ok everyone, let's make a break for the Arrow Tree,
and head back to 1881 where we came from!

TIM MACROY

Dad, I'll stop by where the magic entrance is near
the arrow tree and direct people back home.

JOHN MACROY

Ok son, keep them going out!

TIM MACROY

I got it!

Everyone is following a line going out of 100 million years
ago into modern living 1881. Virginia is walking with baby
to the exit. A large 12-foot snake rears up and blocks the
entrance. Virginia lifts the side of her dress and pulls a snub
nose 45 from her leg holster. BAM! BAM! BAM! BAM!
BAM! BAM! The snake's head blew off and it wiggles in
its blood and guts. Little Ginny is crying. WAA! WAA!

VIRGINIA

Well baby Ginny, it always pays to have a spare pistol.

SGT CONNORS

That's some shooting Virginia!

VIRGINIA

I've done bigger and better shooting in wild west shows.

TIM MACROY
Hurry! Hurry! Bring horse and wagons before
this opening closes!!! Everyone comes!

VIRGINIA

Tim, have you seen the other wagon that my husband, Rod
McCulla and Cookie tried to turn around and join us?

TIM MACROY

I haven't seen them as yet, but Mrs. Virginia I know Rod
McCulla will get them comin' back here right soon. I
guarantee it! Now go through this passage way with little
Ginny. I'll send him right through when they get here.

Everyone speeds through the chasm. A handful of
velociraptors start to attack some of the wounded dinos.
Blue Wolf yells to one brave in Hunkpapa language.

BLUE WOLF

Look out behind you!!!

The brave turns and fires his Winchester Rifle
3 shots and the Raptor went down.

BLUE WOLF (in Lakota language)

Keep your Eyes looking all around you. No dino surprises.

TIM MACROY

Hurry! Bring horses and wagons before this
opening closes.!! Everyone comes!

Blue Wolf and his braves make a barrier to protect those
exiting. One "T" rex charges the Sioux braves.

BLUE WOLF (HUNKPAPA LANGUAGE)

Aim bullets and arrows at his eyes and neck! He is getting
closer. Now let him have it! BAM! BAM! BAM! BAM! BAM!

One eye was shot out by the rifles and the other eye had
two arrows stuck in it. The giant dino limped around
blind and in pain. He fell to the ground. Raptors came
and started to tear him apart and eat the king of dinos.
BLUE WOLF (SPEAKS IN LAKOTA TO INDIANS)

Form a wall as we back up our horses to leave.

One raptor felt their presence and broke off to attack. He
jumped 20 feet in the air toward Blue Wolf. He shot the
raptor 4 times in the neck. BAM! BAM! BAM! BAM! Blood
spurted out of the severed arteries. The raptor took on a
last run at Blue Wolf and his horse backed up and kicked
him 8 feet in the air. He was now dead upon landing.

They all race for the magic passage. Three giant snakes chase
the crowd. Big Ben stands in front of the snakes and points his
Gatling rifle at them. BAM! BAM! BAM! BAM! BAM! BAM!
BAM! BAM! He went through a bandolier of bullets. The snakes
looked like chopped spaghetti and sausage in a red (blood) sauce.

BIG BEN

My family don't like snakes. I hate 'em.

BLUE WOLF (Lokata language to his men)

Retreat through the magic passage. It's time to go
home. Leave now before the opening closes! I go to
find runaway wagon with MacRoy's men on it.
Ben sees the rest of people going through the magic chasm.
He sees Blue Wolf leading a team to find the runaway wagon
that has Rod McCulla, Cookie and Dr. Bernard on it.

The six braves on horseback with Blue Wolf quickly headed
where people and soldiers were almost all out. A screeching
noise came from above. It was a Pterodactyl diving for Raven
Feathers. Two braves stopped their horses and began firing

their rifles at this flying prehistoric giant. BAM! BAM! BAM!
BAM! BAM! The giant flying dino turned around and came
back for another try. BAM! BAM! BAM! The flying Dino was
slightly faltering. Big Ben ran up with his Gatling rifle.

BIG BEN

Now stand back I'm gonna' let him have it!

Rat Tat! Tat! Tat! Tat! Tat! Bam! Bam! Bam! Bam! Bam!
The ugly flying giant lowered his body and flew right into
the arrow tree. His long beak was stuck in the tree.
BIG BEN

Now I'm gonna" call it the FLYING DINO TREE.!

Some of the people laughed- Ha! Ha! Ha!

Ben and Tim see the rest of these remaining
people go through the magic portal.

TIM MACROY

I'm on it, Ben.

BIG BEN

Tim, it's important everyone goes through the magic passage. I
need to go back and find Rod, Cookie, and Dr. Bernard. They
are on that runaway wagon headed toward our last camp.

TIM MACROY

You be careful ya' hear?

BIG BEN

No worries... I be careful. I be talking to
'dose horses cause 'dey listen to me.

TIM MACROY

I should go with you.

BIG BEN

I'll be okay. I'm gonna be walkin' at a steady pace. Now go son and tell everyone Ben is gonna' help the last four of us make it safely back to the T&J Ranch. Now son have the rest of Ya' say a little prayer. We'll be back, I promise!

TIM MACROY

Here is my two revolvers and ammo belt and holsters set. It's big enough for even a fighter's waist.

Tim puts them around his beltline.

BIG BEN

Well, you are right they fit on the last belt hole.

BIG BEN (continued)

Now get through that magic passage!

TIM MACROY

Bye Ben, we'll be waiting for you all!

Tim passes through the magic portal back to the year 1881. He sees everyone that made it back.

PONCHO GARCIA

Hi Mr. Tim. You made it back finally. Where's Big Ben?

TIM MACROY

He stayed to find Rod McCulla, Cookie, and Dr. Bernard and bring the runaway wagon back home. He has to find the wagon first. The horses like Ben. Besides I gave him my revolvers and ammo belt and holsters for his protection.

VIRGINIA

Tim! Tim! Did you see my husband, Dr. Bernard?

TIM MACROY

No Virginia, the doctor, Cookie, and Rod McCulla were trying
to turn around a runaway wagon chased by some dinosaurs.
Everything will go well. Rod and Ben are the best cowboys
for those horses to listen to. They should be back soon.

JOHN MACROY

Tim me boy! (they hug) I'm so glad you're back with the
living. You can ride double back on this horse if you want.
We've got about an hour to get back to the ranch.

SGT. CONNORS

Hi John and Tim. It looks like Tim could use a horse? We
have Major Cole's horse for your use if you want to ride it?

TIM MACROY

Dad, do you think it's alright?

JOHN MACROY

Sure thing my son. If Sgt. Connors said it's
alright, it's just fine with me Tim.

SGT. CONNORS

That's great Tim. Pfc. Farmer could you come here. Our guide
to get us out of dinosaur land, Tim MacRoy, needs a horse.
Please get Major Cole's horse ready to go for Tim to ride.

PFC. FARMER

It will take about 15 minutes, and it's about ready to go.

TIM MACROY

Thank you so much!

JOHN MACROY

Anything I can do for you just tell me. I appreciate this.

SGT. CONNORS

John, you have done so much already.

JOHN MACROY

When we get back to my ranch, you and your men
can take a rest stop and we'll have lunch.

SGT. CONNORS

Sounds good John, Let's do it.

BIG BEN WALKS TOWARD THE MACROY CAMP SITE-DAY
The horse drawn wagon is approaching. Ben sees the wagon
and the horses are pulling at a good pace toward him.

BIG BEN

Hey you all, you got room for this gimpy
legged bare-knuckle fighter?

ROD MCCULLA

I think we do, if you can show us the way
through the magic Passage to 1881.

BIG BEN

I can do that. Help this old warrior to ride up top and
let me talk to my horsey friends. We'll go to the arrow
tree. The new name is the Flying Dino Tree.

ROD MCCULLA

The what?

BIG BEN

Well before I left to come here, we were attacked by this forty- foot
flying dino... It looked like a giant flying bat with a head like a

stork. It started trying to attack us. The regulars and Army soldiers
were firing at him with lower caliber guns. They used Winchester
rifles and the like. I ran and got a Gatling rifle with about 12
bullets left to fire. That flying monster tried a 2nd pass at us. I fired
all I had. He was hurt and crashed into the arrow tree beak first!
Like I said before, its new name is THE FLYING DINO TREE.

COOKIE

Maybe we put up sign pointing this way out. It is same
direction as the flying Dino Bird. Maybe we bring
tourists and we all know where to leave when Dinos
are mean and have bad manners?!!Ha!Ha!Ha!

ROD MCCULLA

Yes, you could be a new comedy team -" Ben and Cookie standup
Comics" Ha! Ha! Ha! What do you think Dr. Bernard?

THERE WAS COMPLETE SILENCE.

ROD MCCULLA

Dr. Bernard wakes up!

Dr. Bernard falls over in the sitting position.

COOKIE

Look what is crawling out of his shirt!

A small brown colored scorpion walks onto the
back of his hand from inside his shirt.

ROD MCCULLA

Cookie, do we have a small jar with a lid on it?

COOKIE

Yes, we do in the wood crate.

Cookie walks over to get it

COOKIE

Here Rod, you have jar and lid.

ROD MCCULLA

Thanks Cookie.

Rod scoops up scorpion and closes the lid. He then feels
Dr. Bernard's head. He is very warm with fever.

ROD MCCULLA

Ben gets us to MacRoy's ranch as quickly as you possibly
can. Cookie gets me that leather doctor's satchel over there.
I need to look for a thermometer and other medicines.

COOKIE

I have bag with doctor's things inside. Look here is a thermometer.
He hands it to Rod.

ROD MCCULLA

The thermometer reads 105 degrees just from inside his
mouth. The doctor is in bad trouble. Cookie, can you give
me a clean rag emersed in water. We must pat his neck and
forehead with water and fan him to cooler temperatures.

BLUE WOLF, RAVEN FEATHERS AND BRAVES

Blue Wolf and braves ride up to the last wagon
and Raven Feathers speaks for Blue Wolf.

Greetings from us to you. The dinosaurs have calmed.
We will escort you to the Macroy Ranch.

ROD MCCULLA

Doctor Bernard has gotten stung by a scorpion and we
are doctoring him on the way back to John's ranch.

RAVEN FEATHERS

We will protect you as we go through the magic passage
to Macroy's Ranch. You go first and we will fight any
Dinos. We will look for milkweed plants on the way.
These have a milk that draws poison out of a sting.

ROD MCCULLA

Ok, Blue Wolf and Raven Feathers, let's get going back to the ranch.

BIG BEN

Rod and Cookie, brother Ben here is gonna' push the horses to
John and Tim's Ranch before you can say black-eyed peas. You hear?
Come on lil' children, Ben is gonna' have all kinds of hay and water
and maybe even some apples for ya'. My babies Uncle Ben is gonna'
treat you special when we get there. Haaaa! Go fasta' my sweeties!

The horses love to work hard for Master Ben.

ROD MCCULLA

How long before we get there Ben?

BIG BEN

We jus' comin' up to the magic passage way. Look! Dere's
the Flying dino stuck in the arrow tree! There's the wavy air.
That's the entrance and we is goin' in to our world. Come on
horsies we's goin' home. Rod, how is the Doctor doin'?

ROC MCCULLA

He is still 105 degrees. I am going to look for some healing drug
in this medicine bag. Okay here is some cough syrup and here
is a menthol rub and here is some aspirin. Here is a bottle of
alcohol. That will help if I rub him down with alcohol and he
takes a couple of aspirins. Ben keeps this rocking wagon goin'

BIG BEN

We passin' through the magic passage right now.

EVERYONE

Yippe! Alright! Now we're gonna make it. Come on
Doctor get yourself back to enjoy everything.

THE INDIANS PROTECT THE REAR OF THE
CONVOY THROUGH THE MAGIC PORTAL

COOKIE

We need for doctor to wake so he has food to get better.

JOHN MACROY

Hi you all! I waited for you here. How is Doctor Bernard
Doing? When we get back to my ranch, we've got to
find some medicine to heal his scorpion bite.

We all can take a rest stop and we'll have lunch.

BIG BEN

Look we're back to the modern world of 1881!

Ben see's Tim was waiting for him and the rest of the gang.

BIG BEN & TIM MACROY

Hooray! Were here! We made it!

Everyone. Army and civilians shout with hearts of joy.
Freedom from Dinosaurs and back to the modern world of
1881. The Army gets ready to March back to their fort.

SGT. CONNORS

John, I want to thank you. We came back peaceful. No
Major Wills. It's a shame we left Major Cole and Pvt.
Meyers bodies behind. They were killed by that maniac
Major Wills. God bless you all MacRoy and crew!!

ARMY PLATOON

Army men shout, Hooray!!! Best to you
all!! Alright we're headed home!

SGT CONNORS

Ok men John invited all of you to his ranch for
lunch. Let's help with what's needed.

JOHN MACROY

I want everyone to rest at my ranch and enjoy the great meal
Cookie will prepare for all of us. That includes the US Army.
May God Bless you all Sgt. Connors and crew! Everyone
in our group listen up! This includes Dr. Adam Bernard,
Virginia and lil' Ginny, Big Ben, Rod McCulla, Hans Becker,
Poncho Garcia, Cookie, all Indians, Blue Wolf, Raven
Feather, Painted horse and the rest of the Sioux braves.

TIM MACROY

Dad, did you forget anyone?

JOHN MACROY

And it includes my son Tim, last but not least.

Everyone claps: yeah, good work Tim!

VIRGINIA

John, could you please bring my husband here? I found
his doctor's bag and it has a Medical Guide Book with
remedies to some bites that includes scorpions.

JOHN MACROY

Rod, could you please have someone help to bring
the doctor here. I have a stretcher in that closet
on the patio. Tim, could you help Rod?

TIM MACROY

I'm a comin'!

A small crowd comes to the master bedroom where
they take the unconscious Doctor Bernard.

VIRGINIA

I have his DOCTOR'S GUIDE BOOK here and it says on
chapter 15, Bites and Remedies. Put cold wet compresses on his
forehead and take his temperature with an oral thermometer.

Tim comes back quickly with a clean wet wash cloth and helps
put it on his forehead while Virginia takes his temperature. His
temperature is 105. Can someone give me a fan to wave air and
cool him down. Thanks Tim. Could you wave a breeze of that
fan on him Tim? Thanks. It says here in this guide book to rub
alcohol on his chest to also help bring down the temperature.
Virginia takes his "t" shirt off and rubs alcohol on his chest.

Blue Wolf heard about the doctor's dilemma and
came with his interpreter - Raven Feathers

BLUE WOLF

Show me where the scorpion stung him. Yes, I see the red mound
where the Scorpion got him. What did the scorpion look like?

ROD MCCULLA

Here is the jar we caught him in. See him he is still
walking around. He's a brown scorpion.

BLUE WOLF

It is good that a white or black scorpion did not sting him.
The brown ones make you sick with fever for a day or two.
When this has happened to someone in our tribal group,
we find milkweed, cut it and apply to the wound after
we cut a slit through the bite. It then heals quickly. Mam
(Virginia) your husband will be alright in about one day.

RAVEN FEATHERS

I have already told Painted Horse and the others to bring
us some milk weed. Here they come with a bundle of
them. They give some nice stalks. I will cut the them to
make the milk flow. I will rub the wound with them.

A small cut is placed through the middle of the stinger wound. Now this milk weed will dry and suck poison from the wound. It's starting to dry and draw the poison.

JOHN MACROY

Such good news. The Doctor is being healed by Sioux medicine men!

VIRGINIA

Let's take his temperature. She puts the thermometer under his tongue. It's 102. He's getting better! Virginia starts crying and so does baby Ginny.

JOHN MACROY

Virginia, I say you stay with Doctor Bernard and Ginny for a while and I'll get Cookie to cook a celebration meal for all of us. Ok?!!VIRGINIA

VIRGINIA

Thank you so very much John!

JOHN MACROY

Now let's all go to the living room patio area. Everyone that signed up for this adventure to find Virginia. All that came on this journey will get $750 to include: my son Tim, Dr. Bernard, Big Ben, Hans Becker, Rod McCulla, Pancho Garcia, and Cookie. Blue Wolf tells your braves that I will reward them later. I know that you will try to find Red Eagle when we finish eating and go our separate ways. You must stay in touch with us. You are always welcome. Raven Feathers, could you come up here close. I am going to keep each braves money in my safe. When you need some of your money you come and I will buy whatever you need. It will be $750 each. Tim will you please get some envelopes and write each Indian's name on the outside and put the money inside. Then put the envelopes in the safe. This way the white man cannot take advantage of your money. We will guard it for you. When you come to me to buy things with it, I will help you to spend your money in town on what you need Now. John talks in regular voice to everyone.

I WANT YOU ALL TO ENJOY YOUR PAY:

I WILL CALL YOU UP HERE INDIVIDUALLY
TO GIVE YOU YOUR REWARD:

Virginia, come on up here. You were responsible for this expedition to find you. Surprise, we found you and your husband Doctor Bernard and baby Ginny. I am giving $750 for each of you. Here take this and put it in a safe place. You can even put it in my safe. I have several private compartments that can easily hold your money, your husband's and Ginny's.

VIRGINIA

(Crying) this means so much to me John. I can't begin to thank you.

JOHN MACROY

Now Mrs. Bernard, don't get this old man crying with the bunch of you. You made it out of Dino -land and we are celebrating our return! Virginia and Ginny wave to all the people as they step down to go back to be with Dr. Bernard.

TIM MACROY

Hey Dad look! Dr Bernard is sitting up and talking with everybody.

DR. BERNARD

What in the world has happened. I left a bad dream about being attacked by Dinosaurs and now I'm in the United States, South Dakota, I think.

JOHN MACROY

Yes, Dr. Bernard you're out of the JUNGLE, and now staying on my ranch in South Dakota and the year is 1881.

DR. BERNARD

Virginia, are you out there?

VIRGINIA

Sweetheart look at you, you're getting better real fast thank to
Rod McCulla, Tim, Cookie, Raven Feathers and Blue Wolf
. I doctored you too! Ha, ha, ha, I sure love you honey!

We are dedicating the rewards to the folks that came to
find us They get $750 for each of them. John already paid
us just before you awoke from that scorpion bite.

JOHN MACROY

Dr. Bernard, Virginia and little Ginny, you are my
houseguests for however long it takes to get Dr. Bernard's
practice running. Our home is your home.

DR. BERNARD

John, thank you so much my kind and loving friend. That solves
a lot of problems. We in turn will help manage your ranch-home
so that we are all conscious of any needs or work that needs to be
done. I will try to run my medical practice such to call on patients
in their homes. That should make things less complicated. I will
see patients here at the ranch only in a life and death situation;

JOHN MACROY

That works for me Dr. Bernard

Dr. Bernard, Virginia and baby mingle
with all the guests before supper.

THE CROWD

Yeah, good luck, love you guys!

JOHN MACROY

Next up is my son Tim. Son could you come up here?!
Tim walks up to stand next to his dad.

JOHN MACROY

Tim you are my own flesh and blood. I can't begin to tell you
how much love and joy has been here with you at my side.

Sniffle, sniffle. Yes, that's right You can see this grown man cry.
Tim here is your pay. (he hands him $750 in cash) I'm sure
you have thought about what you're going to do with it.

TIMOTHY MACROY

I am so glad I have the best dad in the whole wide world! I love you
dad and I've enjoyed every minute we have been together in these
adventures. I will put this money in our safe with my name on the
zipper case. Perhaps I may need it to complete my education.

Tuffy their dog runs up to be with Tim. Arf! Arf!
Well, come on Tuffy jump up here in my arms.

Tuffy jumped up and started licking him in the face,

EVERYONE

Ha, Ha, Ha, I don't think Tuffy is so tough.
Maybe his real name is Fluffy. Ha, Ha, Ha.

JOHN MACROY

Well, Tuffy is part of the family. He really surprised us
when he kept biting a "T" Rex dinosaurs' toe in our
first adventure in 1880 coming back home through the
portal. So, maybe Tuffy should keep his name?

EVERYONE

That is hilarious. He really attacked the King
of dinosaurs? Keep his name -Tuffy.

Horray for Tuffy!

Tuffy barks cause so many called his name. Arf! Arf! Arf!
He finds Tim his master, and they leave the stage area.

JOHN MACROY

Ok. Now I would like to call Big Ben up here. Where are you, Ben?

BIG BEN

I'm right here Mr. MacRoy. I was helpin' Cookie bring up some of the vittles from the cold storage. Here you are Cookie the chicken, noodles, rice and flour; what you asked for.

COOKIE

That's good! Now go talk to John.

BIG BEN

Hi John, I made it.

JOHN MACROY

You surely made it. I have lots of good memories of our travels through the Land of the Dinosaurs in 1880. We made it through the Crazy Professor who tried to kill us all in our first visit. We made through our second visit in this year 1881 when Crazy Army officers Major Wills and Major Cole sent some of the enlisted men out to spy on us. He wanted a reason to kill us. Sorry Sgt. Connors, we didn't know what was going to happen? Crazy Ex Major Wills was always trying to start a fight with common everyday cowboys.

SGT. CONNORS

We all felt the same as you John. Major Wills tried to make Major Cole Attack Your camp and kill anyone in Army or not, that didn't believe in his distorted lies.

BIG BEN

I guess Major Wills is doin' time in Hell. Big Ben closes his hands around his mouth to shout, Major Wills, say hi to Lucifer while you are in hell. Some people are born unkind and unlucky. When Jesus told Judas 'That would be better if he was never born'. I guess Major Wills will have a chance to visit with Judas, Ya Think?

JOHN MACROY

Well Big Ben, you are a man with a big heart. God took you out of slavery so that you might work a real job here on our J&T Ranch. Here is your $750 for helping us find Virginia.

Ben reaches for the envelope of $750 with his name Big Ben on it. Ben reaches out and shakes John's hand.

BIG BEN

I hope I can continue working on the ranch. I might be able to save up money to buy my own ranch someday.

EVERYONE

Hooray! Yippee! That's wonderful!

JOHN MACROY

Next up is Rod McCulla. Rod, would you come up here.

ROD MCCULLA

Hi again Mr. MacRoy.

JOHN MACROY

Rod its always good to see you especially through all the dinosaur challenges. You are quite good with our Winchester rifles and Gatling Rifles. Let's hope we don't have to fight those mean dinosaurs again, but if we did, YOU and Ben would be up on the line with those Gatling rifles. You, Ben and Cookie stopped several of our wagons that dino's were trying to attack our horses. You made quick work and got the horses away from them. Rod here is your $750 and I look forward to you continue working on our "J&T RANCH". They shake hands. Thank you, John.

JOHN MACROY

Thank you, Rod.

Rod finds Cookie to help get all the food organized.

JOHN MACROY

Where is Poncho Garcia? Here! Poncho come on up here and see me.

PONCHO GARCIA

Ok Mr. Macroy, I'm here for you to look at the only
Mexican quick shot artist you had to save the day when
we got in trouble with those Dinosaurs. Mucho problemos
only for a little while. And now we all are here to celebrate
and be merry. Feliz Navidad! Merry Christmas!!!

JOHN MACROY

Poncho, it is so good to see you on my rancho and here's the
$750 I promised. Now you can buy that Rancho in Mexico
you dreamed about with mucho________________you know
mucho______________. Oh si, you mean mucho senioritas.

JOHN MACROY

That's right now take your money here's $750 for your reward in
helping us. We may come to visit your rancho when it's all done?

PONCHO GARCIA

Please do, everyone will be invited!

JOHN MACROY

Now we have a man who knows how to repair almost any revolver
or rifle out there. Hans Becker will you come up here and get that
hard earned $750 you earned fixing and repairing our shooters.

HANS BECKER

Thank you, John for giving me the opportunity to be a
part of your mission to find Virginia in Dinosaur land.
We had our challenges, but by the grace of God we
found her and made it out of prehistoric earth.

JOHN MACROY

Here you are Hans, $750 that I promised. I hear you
are moving back to Pittsburgh, Pennsylvania. Enjoy
your journey to be with your family back there.

HANS BECKER

Thank you so much John. I really miss my wife Margaret
and my six kids. Margaret sent me a letter 4 months ago.
She and the kids' clean houses to make money to live on.
She will be surprised with the money I have earned. I can't
wait to show her. Maybe we can buy a house. John you are
a man of your word. God Bless you and your family.

JOHN MACROY

Now we have another tremendous man who makes it to all
the challenges and keeps our food coming. Delicious foods
he prepares and glows with the reward that he can makes
exquisite dishes. It's time for Cookie to make his appearance
up here before we serve his world re-known cuisine.
Cookie come on up here. Please Cookie come up here!

COOKIE

(He comes over to see John MacRoy). I jus' wanted to know how
you liked my stew that I cooked for everyone in dinosaur land.

EVERYONE

Cookie it was great. Best I ever had. Beats mom's cooking.

COOKIE

Good Chinese make best cooks. I used 100 million years
old dinosaur steaks you shot and added lots of Chinese
spices, carrots, cabbage, noodles and potatoes.

EVERYONE

We all ate dinosaurs?! HA! HA! HA! HA!

JOHN MACROY

Well, I'll be a monkey's uncle!

COOKIE

No monkies, Jus' Dinosaurs! Today we are back home and Cookie will make a final dinner: chop suey with Chinese noodles, egg rolls, brown rice, chicken and cabbage soup......you like?

Cookie began to tell a handful of people what he needed to get this Chinese banquet going.

EVERONE

We'll help. You bet! Sounds great! I can't wait! Just tell us what you want and we'll get it for you.

JOHN MACROY

We have a cold room in the basement. We have fresh cleaned chicken, cabbage noodles and eggrolls rice and other things to choose from. Cookie, could you go down to our cool/ ice room to pick whatever you like for our final meal tonight. Take as many people as you need to help.

COOKIE

I already using Tim, Virginia, Ben, and another volunteer to get what I need to cook. They had four volunteers

Everyone worked together. They set two large tables, filled pitchers of fresh water, put entrees on both sides of the tables Cookie kept the food coming. He made stove top dishes with chicken and rice and also Chinese noodles. You could smell the fried egg rolls. And cabbage soup. It is grand.

Doctor Bernard is waking up and feeling better.

DR. BERNARD

Wow something smells so good and I sure am hungry!

VIRGINIA

My love you are back with the living. You survived a scorpion bite. Everyone helped you to recover. The Indians also helped big time. We all made it through the time portal and we are here in 1881. Thanks to John and his crew, the U.S. ARMY and Blue Wolf, Raven Feathers and the rest of the Sioux braves.

DOCTOR BERNARD

How long have I been out of it?

VIRGINIA

Well, you had a brown scorpion climbed up your sleeve. It stung you such that you never said anything. I'm thinking you got bit when you turned the wagon around about 3 to 4 hours ago. You never felt it I surmise. Your other cowboy buddies: Big Ben, Rod McCulla & Cookie got a thermometer out of your medical case and we followed instructions to reduce your 105-degree fever. Blue Wolf and Raven Feathers lanced the scorpion sting and got some milk weed to draw out the poison when you got here.

JOHN MACROY

Dr. Bernard we are so happy you are back with the living. There was a moment in time you were living on a wish and a prayer.

ROD MCCULLA

I have seen people die from a scorpion sting in Australia. We have lots of poisonous insects and animals. You can honestly say that you were blessed. The doctor's patients became the Doctors and Healers. God Bless you Doctor Bernard and Virginia and Ginny. This is a happy time for you and all of us!

SGT.CONNORS

This is really a thing of beauty. All my men make sure you offer our helping hand. John MacRoy's people and my talented Army are making a new example of working together.

EVERYONE ENJOYED THEIR FINAL MEAL TOGETHER.

Hooray, yippee, Way to Go!
Just as the meal was culminating and everyone preparing to
go their separate way, two Sioux Indians came up the drive

to the ranch. It was Little Turtle and Chief Red Eagle. Raven Feathers quickly ran out to meet them with Blue Wolf.

LITTLE TURTLE

We are so glad we listened to other braves at the camp that told us the best directions to get to Macroy's Ranch. We had to sneak out of the stockade encampment at night. We waited near our painted ponies and other braves called the soldiers over to see some jackets they had made. They didn't see us with help from our Indian brothers. Raven Feathers continues to be the interpreter.

RED EAGLE

I have been young and now am old like a great mountain goat. I no longer fight with the younger goats. I have but a short moment to give back to my people. My son Blue Wolf you are a glowing example of this old man's purpose in life.

Blue Wolf hugs his dad Red Eagle.

RED EAGLE Blue Wolf you are not afraid to fight for what is good and profitable to bring peace to the Sioux. We do not want to fight with the white man but hope we can live together. I see a vision of settlers moving through-out the West. It will take many to get peaceful living happening.

JOHN MACROY

Greetings Chief Red Eagle. Welcome to my humble ranch. Please take a seat over here with your Sioux braves. Cookie, will you help give food and drinks to these Indians who come in peace. We have been celebrating our return from the land of dinosaurs. These Monsters have stopped us from returning to this time (1881) until we learned how to fight them. We learned to fight them together- Cowboys, Indians, Army and people from other countries. We all fought together. Blue Wolf is our hero. Our large blackman, Big Ben, has been a lead fighter for the past two years.

JOHN MACROY (CONT.)

Our Chinese cook, named -Cookie, knows how to make great meals and knows how to shoot Dinosaurs. Our Australian cowboy,

Rod McCulla, has been a man from 'Downunder", a cowboy from
Australia, on the other side of the world. He can fight with a gun,
a rifle or a boomerang. Poncho Garcia, a Mexican Cowboy, knows
how to shoot fast and stay alive. We have a German firearms expert,
Hans Becker, who can take a pistol apart to fix, clean and back
together in 3 minutes. We are an Army of different people from all
over the world. I am sorry for talking so long Chief Red Eagle.

COOKIE

I put a lot on the Indians' plates chop, chop, fast, fast. They are
eating all gone as we speak the army personnel with Sgt. Connors
were told be good at helping this bunch of braves. They served them
very good, chop! chop! The Army ate their food too. Quick! Quick!

RAVEN FEATHERS

Sioux tribal followers here come and circle around
Red Eagle. This will be a small powwow with all tribal
members that are here at John MacRoys' and John's
Cowboys... Please come here around Chief Red Eagle.

All Sioux circled around the chief cross legged for their
powwow. All Sioux at John Macroy's Ranch received their
chow and drink. John MacRoy, Tim MacRoy, Rod McCulla,
Cookie, Big Ben, Poncho Garcia, Virginia and lil'Ginny
and Dr. Bernard, and Hans Becker, also attended.

BLUE WOLF

Father, I want you and Little Turtle and the rest of our braves
who are here, to stay and visit for 3 days. We must bond
together and learn about how the world needs to get together.
We need to learn how to share our best tools. We need to
speak up to those who need protection and share our treasures
of knowledge for all those good peoples left in the world.

RAVEN FEATHERS

John, we have been talking about how all these different
people of the world can work together for a common good.
We would like to stay here for three more days, to exchange

knowledge and learn the ways of the Great Father of Heaven and Earth. The Army Sargeant what is his name?

JOHN MCROY

His name is Sargeant Connors. Let me ask him to come over here for a spell. Sergeant, could you come here for a brief meeting?

SGT. CONNORS

Be happy to John.

JOHN MACROY

As you can see, we have a handful of Sioux here that have helped us tremendously in our fight against the monster Dinosaurs who prevented us to return to our modern days of 1891. With the help of all our fighters: Your Army, Our Sioux, Our Chinaman (Cookie), Our Australian Cowboy, our Mexican cowboy, our Black gunfighter, and German gunsmith we have prevailed. We lived to tell the story. Sgt. Connors we would love to have you talk with our Indian friends here before you return to your stockade fort up north. Some of your Indians have come down here. Red Eagle the chief is right here (They shake hands)

RED EAGLE

I am glad to see my only son, BLUE WOLF, and talk with him before I go to the Happy Hunting Grounds. I do not know when. I dreamed I will spend three days with him here and I will leave to see a great chief of heaven and earth.

SGT. CONNORS

I can see why you should stay here at John's Ranch for another 3 days. Then you must travel back to the northern stockade. How does that sound to you John?

JOHN MACROY

I like the way we can fellowship and return back to our normal lives. We are back in the real world of 1881 and taking part in those things in life that make us who we are.

RED EAGLE

I remember as a young boy chasing rabbits and learning how to hunt them. We young boys would sneak up on them with a couple rocks in our hands. We were excited to throw and we missed the first couple of times. My third try, knocked one out and my father Big Bear showed me how to skin him and clean the guts from the meat. I was beGinnyng to understand some aspects of life. My father made me a bow and arrows when I was12 years old. He went on a deer hunt with me and showed me how to be ready to shoot my arrow into the heart of the deer. I missed my first try, but my father stayed with me and told me I will get my deer this next time. We tracked him down wind with the breeze blowing our smell away from the deer. We hid in the bushes so well the deer could not see us. I slowly arose with my arrow ready to shoot. Bing!! The arrow left the string and entered the heart area. The deer went down. It was my first deer kill. My Dad, Big Bear, showed me how to butcher and remove the hide. I felt so proud when we returned home to show everyone. Eating my own deer kill was so wonderful. My father was so patient and a great hunter/teacher. I hope I taught Blue Wolf all that he needed in his growing years.

BLUE WOLF

Father, my memories of you taking me fishing when I was about eight years old. We tied a rope to our circular net and carried it to the river. We found a spot where the fish were jumping in a river pool. Father did you remember what happened when I took the rope hoop and threw the circular net out there as hard as I could.

RED EAGLE

You did not get the net in the water?

BLUE WOLF

Correct! I caught the tree branch. I had to climb out on the branch with you carrying me to get up there.

RED EAGLE

Ha, Ha, Ha and after you got it you threw it to me and you fell into the river. Ha, Ha, Ha!

EVERYONE

Ha, Ha, Ha, Ha, Ha,

BLUE WOLF

Do you remember I got better throwing the net and we went with
Eight nice fish we ate when we got home. Mom was laughing
when you told her how I fell out of the tree branch trying to
get the net out. Later you took me to learn how to hunt the
MENETONKA (Buffalo). The bow and arrow we used were very
hard to pull back and fire. I had to learn by shooting dead trees.

RED EAGLE

You became very good Blue Wolf. I loved when you finally
took your best braves to hunt the MENETONKA. Our
village ate wonderful meat steaks. The women made
Buffalo blankets from the hides for the winter months.

BLUE WOLF

I was doing great hunting TETONKA until a weird three
horned white bull attacked us and I chased him back into a
dinosaur land. All of the men in this room fought the dinosaurs
and we all helped each other. We made it back to 1881.

RED EAGLE

I was very sad to tell you about your mother, Summer Flower,
passing away. You were lost for almost seven months. Your
mother was sick with fever she caught while worrying about
you being missing. I know it was hard on you when you
returned. You know how much she loved you, her only child.

BLUE WOLF

Dad, I have prayed to the great heavenly father and hope I
can find a woman to be my wife that reflects all the wonderful
ways of my mother, Summer Flower. I believe I will find her.

RED EAGLE

I will pray you do. Your mother in heaven is
looking for your mate to find you.

JOHN MACROY

I will pray My mother finds me a wife also.

EVERYONE

Ha, ha, ha, ha,

JOHN MACROY

No, I'm really serious. I lost my opportunity with Virginia; she's
married to Dr. Bernard. I am happy for them, believe me.

VIRGINIA

John, I will keep my eyes and ears open. I know the
kind of woman for you. Just hang in there. Ok?

JOHN MACROY

Ok Virginia I receive that. I'M sorry Red Eagle. We
have a bunch of lonely guys here, I guess.

RED EAGLE

It is now different for me. I do not look for a replacement for
Summer Flower, I look forward to meeting up with her in the
Happy Hunting Ground. She and I will continue forever.

EVERYONE

Hooray! You will see Summer Flower. It's bound to happen! It's
meant to be! Many people in the meeting room were crying
tears of joy. Red Eagle bowed his head between his knees.

SGT. CONNORS

Well Red Eagle this has been an extraordinary time
together. I glad we have the opportunity to go back
with the Sioux that are here in two more days.

RAVEN FEATHERS

(He walks over to where the Chief is sitting). Red Eagle!
Do you hear me? Are you awake? DOCTOR. Can
you come and see if our chief is still with us?

DR. BERNARD

Virginia, could you please get my doctor's black bag for me?

VIRGINIA

Yes, honey I'll be right back. She runs quickly and gives
the medicine bag and Doctors things to Dr. Bernard.

Dr. Bernard checks his pulse on his veins, no pulse was detected.
He checked his eyes for response to light. No response was detected.

DR. BERNARD

It appears that Red Eagle has just departed. He is not alive in
our world. I can see him walking to meet Summer Flower his
sweetheart in the other life. The Happy Hunting Grounds perhaps.

EVERYONE (crying)

Blue Wolf came up to hold his father. He was happy for his dad.
BLUE WOLF Father, you taught me so much about life. I know
you will continue with my mother, Summer Flower. Hug her for
me too. I will make you and mother proud, as I learn about this
world. Good Journeys to you both, all my love I send to you always.

JOHN MACROY (He walks up to talk to Red Eagle)

Red eagle, I remember meeting you at the Pow Wow a little more
than a year ago... I was there to get your permission to search
for Blue Wolf in the land of the dinosaurs. I knew we could find
Blue Wolf if we could find the magic portal to Dinosaur land.
We had the weapons, the supplies and the determination to
win. We found your son and the Sioux Braves that accompanied
us. Everyone helped to kill the white dinosaur and proceed
out of Dinosaur World. It was a great fight with all the Lizard-
like monsters that attacked us. We won at the end. I kept my

promise and saved your son with the help of all that rode in to fight these Dino creatures. Enjoy your time in the happy hunting ground. Hug and kiss Summer Flower while you're there!

RAVEN FEATHERS

Chief Red Eagle, I am here at John MacRoy's ranch to speak for The Sioux. We will miss you Greatly. Please think about the Sioux that we make good decisions for the times ahead.

SGT. CONNORS

I must talk about our situation. We must bury the chief or take him to the wilderness and build a burial stand. What do you suppose we do? Could you find out Raven Feathers.

JOHN MCROY

I buried my wife, Rachel, in a plot in the back yard. He is welcome to be buried below her plot. I will save my plot next to her on the right, my son will have the plot next to her on the left. We will leave room for Blue Wolf in a plot on your right. How does all this sound to you Blue Wolf?

BLUE WOLF (through Raven Feathers)

My good friend and fellow Hunter John MacRoy. I accept your offer for my father to be buried and at rest here my good friends. We hope Sgt. Connors will allow us to stay her two more days for us to bury Red Eagle with our burial dancing and celebration.

JOHN MACROY

I don't see anything wrong with that do you Sgt. Connors?

SGT. CONNORS

John it's all good. Raven Feathers it is good to celebrate Red Eagle's passing to the Happy Hunting Ground.

RAVEN FEATHERS

We will prepare to chant, sing and dance to have the spirits
of our ancestors welcome him to his heavenly home.

COOKIE

I will fix good things to eat in next two days. You like
a lot. Chicken with rice and vegetable soup. Corn and
vegetables of many kinds. You like big time!

JOHN MACROY

So, let's get started.

THE INDIANS LEAD SIOUX TRIBAL
DANCING FOR RED EAGLE

All of the burial tribesmen dug and prepared the plot deep enough
for Red Eagle in his burial clothes. The Army men put much of the
soil about 10 feet away This would be used to fill holes in the ground
for easier wagon riding. The burial was complete. The Indians put on
their dancing garb with feathers and dancing poles. Their drum they
beat told a story. They sang and kept dancing to and fro round and
round. You could visualize Red Eagle walking through a heavenly gate.
There to meet him was his spouse, Summer Flower. Everyone at the
celebration enjoyed talking to one another. Raven Feathers helped to
interpret for the questions about Red Eagle and the Happy Hunting
Ground. The day became Night and two more days past. Blue Wolf
and Raven Feathers were allowed to stay at John Macroy's. They
needed to discuss things with John Macroy about him learning English
to further his Education. Sgt. Connors agreed with the condition
that John would be overseeing the two braves. The other braves
returned to the stockade with Sgt. Connors and the Army Troops.
All went their separate ways: The Army to its' fort, and the Indians to
their village in the fort. Cookie found a spot for his Chinese restaurant
and a home for his wife and baby in Whiskey Creek. Poncho Garcia
bought a Rancho in Mexico. Hans Becker returned to Pennsylvania
with his wife and children. John and Tim Macroy stayed on their
ranch with two of their favorite cowboys- Big Ben and Rod McCulla.
Virginia, little Ginny and Dr. Bernard stayed at John's Ranch for as
long as they wanted. It seemed like everything was working out.

ALL WERE ONE BIG HAPPY FAMILY BACK
IN THE MODERN WORLD OF 1881!